finding theodore and Brina

finding Theodore and Brina

Terri-ann White

FREMANTLE ARTS CENTRE PRESS

First published 2001 by
FREMANTLE ARTS CENTRE PRESS
25 Quarry Street, Fremantle
(PO Box 158, North Fremantle 6159)
Western Australia.
www.facp.iinet.net.au

Production Coordinator Cate Sutherland.
Cover Designer Marion Duke.
Typeset by Fremantle Arts Centre Press
and printed by Lamb Print.

National Library of Australia
Cataloguing-in-publication data

White, Terri-ann, 1959- .
Finding Theodore and Brina.

ISBN 1 86368 337 2.

I. Title.

A823.3

The State of Western Australia has made an investment in this project through ArtsWA in association with the Lotteries Commission.

Publication of this title was assisted by the Commonwealth Government through the Australia Council, its arts funding and advisory body.

for
Roy Rivers White
and Marlena Ann White
beloved nephew and niece

Contents

The dead have a power over the living. There are rituals to placate them and prayers to succor them. Sometimes the living can supplicate the dead, requesting help in this world and intervention from the powers above. Wherever the dead reside, in some heavenly kingdom or in earthly graves, their presence is felt by the living, and it is through the living that they find a measure of eternal life.

Kugelmass and Boyarin, *From a Ruined Garden*

There is a fact of life in a country with a small population: everyone over thirty knows everyone else. Either you have grown up with them or played sports against them or taken them to dances or made love to them. And now there they are — in government or in jail or anchoring the television news.

Robert Drewe, *Fortune*

There is no such thing as society; there are only individuals and their families.

widely attributed to former British
Prime Minister Margaret Thatcher
(claimed by her to be imprecise reporting)

finding theodore and Brina

in other places

We learn landscape through love. The physical spaces and our own thresholds of pleasure merge and proffer all manner of things: sensations, stored expectations, moments with sharp edges. I am with her in a new place, another city: neither mine nor hers. We explore it on our bicycles together, and each day when she is at her new workplace and I am pretending to write I ride and practise the places and routes I can show her. Not one-upmanship, but always presented as a gift. In the early evenings and on weekends we ride together, me a little way behind because I do not have her fitness or courage.

In preparation for this journey she has read the maps and still she navigates us into dead ends: a river path that disappears and leaves us far from our destination. I am dressed up, ridiculously, with high heels and a skirt split right to the middle of my thigh. The skirt billows out, and each time she turns around to check on me she exclaims something under her breath. For her, cycling has always been an exercise; in our new city it is our only mode of transport. I want to make a good first impression.

Here I am a little way into the future already admonishing her. She was as nervous as me at this time of transition in our love affair.

The river banks are so lush and still and so unlike Perth. Riding along the path, we see all manner of life but only twice do we have to cross over roads and watch for cars. And we have been riding now for thirty minutes. There is still plenty of sharp sun in the sky and it is burning down on me, and I feel my nose and my thigh burning slightly. Later it will rain and soak us through on our shorter ride home through city streets. We are here, together, against all sorts of obstacles, and are attempting to make a life together. This seeming image of Arcadia makes us anew, almost; alienated from the familiar, able in many ways to think straight, we are together and, mostly, happy.

My memory holds and is haunted by minute moments and habits, stumbling upon scenes of regret and many dead ends: lunacy, a good old-fashioned word. Through memory developing a map of Perth — the place of childhood and growing, remembered through taste, touch, smell, sight, and sometimes an uncanny luck. Stretching out beyond the influence of original family, that first set of individuals, and into a wider idea of community. Places marked out with impressions, imprints that last while you are anywhere else.

Every place reminds me of you.

What does it mean when one landscape stands in for another? A family holiday in East Timor when I was a child, a formative experience, is played over again and again as an adult back in Perth. On that little plane from Darwin, in 1969, going to an island where the Portuguese are still the colonisers. The young men performing their national service are languid and lazy as my father remembers his national service on another island, Rottnest, just off Fremantle. I've forgotten much more than I lost: the postcards remain as a potent guide across the rest of my life. This holiday changed everything; only it will take years before that change can be properly measured. What difference does Dili have from Perth? It has more hills than the flat suburbs of Perth, bleached by the sun, filled with bland houses, coloured sand and terracotta, and possessed of huge sprawling shopping centres. How are these two places related beyond both being remembered by a ten-year-old girl?

I am gesturing towards an autobiography of place, of marking out Perth as geography worth something. My body in Perth, I concentrate my vision out, and beyond.

Every place reminds me of home.

Would this dislocation of mine, this filtered vision, have been so powerful if contemporary politics hadn't made East Timor, our near neighbours, such a focus of shame? If, since 1975, there hadn't been human rights contraventions reported, film footage of deprivations, atrocities, resistance? Would I have remembered the holiday in East Timor in an exotic way but largely through the reference point of family? Remembered simply: through the precious yellow box of Kodak slides, the batiks I draped over sofas and beds, the anecdotes of the wild adventures of two little girls and their parents, a neat family?

Until I was an adult I didn't look at the landscape. It appeared to me as the filler on the way to somewhere. And when I turned and began to see, I was astonished by how thoroughly made it was, by the gradations of colour, the disarray that was allowed to continue to exist; by the way the light fell and illuminated trees, spinifex, grasses. Rolling plains of green or brown. Rocky outcrops.

Everything reminds me.

All I really want to do is make a picture of a body passing through a life with the requisite joy. The pleasure of holding the ankle of a beloved by simply curving your hand around it, of burying a parent at the end of his long and satisfied life. Of having one set of people stand in for another: friends and lovers for family, or the other way around. Place and people as intertwined, as the material of satisfaction.

If you haven't been to Perth you won't know about the Swan River. It is late in the day when I remember. I drive this way out of habit every single day of the week so this time I decide to look. The best time all year round is just before six, almost night but still it is light. There are people walking together and sometimes they are clipped by waves that come from nowhere. They are self-contained, these waves; they happen rarely and are not part of any series. The river is fairly flat.

In this space of pondering about why we follow paths and patterns of work, intellectual pursuits, love, romance and solitude, I wonder, is it all one or the other, either luck or planning; is there no in between? No room for the decision made in extreme circumstances, the decision that affects everything, that leaves you without a chance of getting back to where you were. Which, on reflection, might be a better place, but it is not the place you chose.

Driving around this river, on the rump of land, on the winding road between escarpment and water. The light leaving the sky slowly, the water glistening. The sky leached of all late-day colour is the palest shade of … what? How could it be described? As if in a dream, it's so soft you could wrap yourself in it because you have never seen anything so extraordinary. A shade of salmon, but not pink.

presently

monuments

The years slip around and can be difficult to place, to keep as a chronology. 1874. 1893. 1993. Now. Back to where it all started: 1851 and 1853. The site of convergence is just off the road that runs into Broomehill, Western Australia.

On the side of the road just before the town centre, on the right as you drive in from Katanning heading north-east, there is this grand monument to pioneering days:

Erected By The
Katanning Branch
Of The
W.A. Historical Society
To Commemorate The
Epic Journey Of

John Holland
(Leader)
Rudolph Krakour
David Krakour
And John Carmody
Who Pioneered The Road
From Broomehill
To Coolgardie
Known As
HOLLANDS TRACK
14th April–18th June
1893

Once you have driven into the town you will be prepared for every other part of the Wheatbelt region: flat pastures, colours without any real vibrancy, farmhouses and evidence of rural industry within sight of the straight road.

In an imaginative flourish I project myself into a meeting of family around the monument in this town. The two Jewish men named on the monument and their brothers are some of the nine children born in Fremantle between 1853 and 1869 of parents who had been born in Europe, one in Krakow and one in London. Their father's name was Krakouer and, while the monument has been engraved with an incorrect spelling, they know what their name means: *Of Krakow.* The men know their roots, their lineage, that they are Jews at the end of a long line of peoples. They know that their birth in this place, Western Australia, has marked a shift in the fortunes of the family. A shift not of wealth but of belonging. Their parents had said to them: *This can be your homeland if you choose it.* Registered safely into the records of the colony, owning property and having a vote, none of them will have the chance to continue the long Jewish family line. All of the men will marry gentiles, and none of their children will consider themselves to be Jewish.

Born of a pure union in the Swan River Colony in the middle of its first white century, they will be the last generation of Jews in the family.

One set of peoples is displaced by another. There is an imperative here around homelands, an imperative of possession, of symbolic ownership and rights. Sons of a Jewish convict make their way warily in this community and, following the practices of the day, some of them have sexual relations with Nyoongar women. Such contact with indigenous women is well documented as a regular pastime of settler men in the colony, although still rarely discussed. Official documents cannot record the nature of these relations: whether or not they involved love and affection, whether they were a perverse manifestation of the desire for assimilation, part of the national project of addressing the problem of the "coloured minority",[1] or whether the sexual congress could be named as rape.

In the farmhouse just out of Broomehill the young brothers gather for their Friday night ritual. They improvise but that is easy because they have known how to do these prayers all of their lives. The *Minyan* of ten men required to conduct prayers and services has never been possible, but their father had instructed them on matters of living and following *Halacha* and had given them many words and concepts for the Sabbath so they could live as righteous Jews. They keep quiet about their practices in Broomehill and in the other towns they have lived in. Stay quiet, too, in the face of any resistance from the families of the women they married. There is enough to think about in a life without worrying about private beliefs and prayer.

If the Nyoongar members of the family arrive to meet around this monument at the designated hour, will they be accepted or even acknowledged? Depending upon the year of the meeting, they may be rounded up and transported to a mission like Mogumber at Moore River as part of the containment policies formulated to counter the "coloured problem". They may simply be shooed away by the "real" family. Or, after the brilliant success of two brothers in the national Australian Rules football competition in the 1980s, they may be welcomed cautiously as the most famous and well-known of the Krakouers in Australia, as sporting icons in a nation that takes such athletic prowess and fighting spirit seriously.

The meeting won't happen. There have been attempts in the past but there are too many differences and too many exclusions have already been enforced. It cannot happen except in my head. And so, here am I. The keeper of secrets, the family archivist, hiding behind a signature and a barrage of words, holding my own silences. The gaps are what drives this storytelling of an Australian family that is five generations old.

From the vantage point of this moment in our history, the shame that has not been spoken is only of the most ordinary variety. Nothing at all to distinguish it from all of those other mistakes out in the world. But once avoidance is installed, amnesia is the usual outcome, and then the mere echo of any detailed data, spoken out loud, can send a shiver right through any collection of individuals.

I have learnt well and thoroughly from the keeping of these family treasures. Mine are kept in locked boxes and, in there, become puzzles. By the time I am dead they will be incomprehensible, written in code to keep all of my tracks covered. Even if the basic details are understandable, that *I loved deeply* and *they said I was a generous lover*, nothing will be enunciated for a general readership, for the uninitiated. What is left at the end of a life? To sift through the evidence will not yield much. Am I writing the family story as a compensation for the secrets of locked boxes, the unspoken; is this a different form of recording? Foregoing my place in the evolving family. But if this family did not pass down anything, then what are we left with anyway? Nothing. I am left with a yearning involving memory traces, no substance; requiring me to make what I can of apparitions. I have a keen knowledge of the nature of apparitions.

Perth: sketching a past

Captain James Stirling and the Colonial Botanist of New South Wales, Charles Fraser, landed at the Swan River in 1827 and, after exploring the river and the foothills of the Darling Ranges, described the landscape in this way:

> The richness of the soil, the bright foliage of the shrubs, the majesty of the surrounding trees, the abrupt and red-coloured banks of the river occasionally seen, and the view of the blue summits of the mountains from which we were not far distant, made the scenery round this spot as beautiful as anything of the kind I had ever witnessed.[2]

Driving around the river again — it's not so hard, as the river runs through Perth and down to Fremantle — I hook into a mood, an incipient fear. Isolation, the favourite myth, strikes in our bellies and changes us. We sit here upon the landscape, on the edge of this dryness, looking out onto the Indian Ocean. Water and heat. The perils of the encroaching outback and the day-after-day reports of how much water is in the dams and how much is required; it is no wonder we talk about the weather so much. But then there is this luminous body: the river sparkling, even at the end of a winter day.

So the first thing to consider is the heat of a Perth summer, a furnace. With a slow build, too, usually, so that by the time you anticipate autumn softness it has reached a climax. Day after day of profound heat.

Smoke comes down onto the city during the summer and we are easily submerged. This hot place, a land of little water, by now we should be used to the panic. But it is hard when houses go and firefighters burn to death, the city under siege. A sense of calm is difficult to maintain, living each day becomes a strain. In the face of this heat we rely upon the myth making of a land of plenty, on its abundance, an improvement on Europe, the enterprise and the brilliant foresight of the British Establishment. The initiatives of the penal system and the transportation of free settlers to places outside Europe: to Canada, to Australia; new colonies with much more space, fresh air; a different form of plenitude.

I feel mortality on my skin; I wear it and it encloses me. Not oppressive, but redolent and reverent. People have come before me. The cloak serves to protect and to remind me of real pleasure, of acquaintance, of intimacies that follow friendship and love and which make a richer life.

The story you are entering contains people in a place, this hot place, home to a family for a century and a half. Men in Sydney say to me, this she who carries the story through her signature, that it must be because of a surprising family background, my *blood*, that I have such good skin — well suited to any climate, flawless. Well, they go on a bit too much and spoil the first flattering effect.

Our Jewish forebears used incantations to remember the dead. Nowadays we swallow names. Stay silent. Implode with our knowledge of specific pain and what is no longer there.

Laying down the tracks. First, the records kept simply for the sake of it. Births, deaths, marriages, property transactions. Only in the future do these records gain their proper value. Then the remembrance of those times lived, held by the people who lived them. Then the realm of fantasy, the imagined olden days. Next, interpretation, a revisiting, an attempt to understand where this family came from, and how we have each moved through the world. The trails eventually covered over, by neglect, by lack of respect, by shame, by sheer indifference. Start digging and there is plenty, even though it is never enough. This is a different register of information. What is found is what is not there: the hushed-over space of mistakes and shameful wrong turns; lost items, including the lives of individuals not deemed interesting enough to preserve.

Hard to beat the power of the words on the Certificate of Lunacy of Theodore Krakouer, my grandmother's grandfather, signed by the Medical Superintendent of Fremantle, H C Barnett, in 1873 when the patient was in his late fifties. He was suffering from delusions: he was in a state of delusional excitement, telling the doctor that *he hears a voice operating from his belly giving him messages from God Almighty to destroy the world.* His death certificate four years later gives cause of death as *Softening of the Brain, Paralysis and Exhaustion.*

grandparents

Theodore Krakouer, arrived in Perth, then the Swan River Colony, in 1851, twenty-two years after the British invaded and made a fledgling free town. He arrived as a convict on the *Mermaid.* He was already married, he had a son, he had had a variety of occupations, including wool sorter, and had been convicted of stealing clothes and money. He spent time in Portsmouth Gaol before making the journey to Fremantle. He was literate, a Jew, and his convict papers declared that his state of mind was *hopeful.*

Brina Israel, my grandmother's grandmother, arrived two years later by her own volition. With her sister Esther she made the remarkable choice to leave London and its community of Jews to start a new life in this colony so far from her home. She was an unmarried emigrant woman on supported passage to a colony that wanted domestic servants and wives for its male population.

These two people in Perth in the middle of the nineteenth century, categorised in the language of that century's census-keeping as *Jews Mahomedans and Infidels*.[3] There was just a handful of Jews here then, not enough for coherence or community. The congregation wasn't founded until 1892, when a handsome synagogue was built in Brisbane Street near the city. Until then there were only small family units and a few convicts, Jews from different classes, some of them here since 1829, the first year of the colony. Their faith contained within their isolation.

I have no access to an Old World: I am Australian, five generations Australian on this side, even more established on my father's side. I am well aware of the dangers of desiring a dramatic family biography. But there are scant records — births, no marriages, a few deaths. I'm not a Jew like them, except in the flimsiest way: with my yearnings, my imaginings of a line made along the maternal, beginning with the pure union of Theodore and Brina. I don't want to forget Theodore and Brina but it appears that everybody else in the world already has.

The names, for me, are now incantations. Theodore Krakouer. Brina Israel. Sometimes it seems that your names are all I have of your lives. Records of you contain physical descriptions and a flamboyant scope for spelling your names — so changeable it disarms me, and makes me even more suspicious of official record keeping.

Will I make up characters to fit what I want from you? My worthy, honourable, pioneering great-great-grandparents?

sketching a present

There is a tradition in this place, entrenched, and well accepted. It starts in 1829 and churns along all of the years. Favours in the tight little system of established business and power. Still as potent as it was with the families who shared the first schemes and opportunities, and made sure that they had a voice into the future. This tradition works across party political lines, across ideological divides. It transcends politics.

It was a very small place for a long time. A failed agricultural colony because not enough capital was risked to push it over the line and make it viable. And maybe they thought they could do things with the land without having completed adequate research. In the initial arrangement for settlement in 1829, the British government gave forty acres of land for every three pounds of capital brought into the country. This was taken up by people who, some of them, had no experience of farming and certainly no experience of being pioneers. This is probably why they came with shiploads of furniture and effects and no idea of the land or what was in store for them.

The government allowed their three pounds of capital to be in kind, and not just cash. By 1831, the allotment was reduced by half, as grand pianos and other marks of wealth and refinement, shipped across the seas, rotted on the shores where they had been off-loaded. Thomas Peel, the instigator of the scheme for a colony, could not convince his wife and daughters to stay in the colony and only stayed himself because he had sunk all of his money into what had been his dream. It was a disaster; from a population of four thousand in 1830, the colony's numbers declined in the next two years to one thousand five hundred.

Then came the gold that meant growth and prosperity, and the other minerals — a mineral wealth, the wealth from underground that has sustained us into another century. Up above ground tearing down the old for the new, over and again.

~

Perth is the ultimate provincial city, *the most isolated city in the world*, a place people escape from as soon as they can. All of my generation desired to leave the moment they were old enough to go somewhere more authentic, bigger, more exciting, where family wasn't: London, Sydney, Melbourne, New York. Utopia for those not born here, for those who choose Perth for its distance from everywhere else, for its wide-open roads and plains. But a burden for the native-born who senses that time is being wasted and real life should commence. Some of these people call Perth *Toy Town.* Most of my family has stayed, lived and died within State borders. Is it an unconscious recognition of the hardships of ancestors keeping us here, or a fear rooting us to what we know, what we think we *are*?

The stories my family told about themselves and how they came to be in this place. Well, they didn't: they told no stories beyond those of kitchen cupboards, lost fortunes, bus timetables, the sanctity of silence in families, the shame of remembering so little.

It starts with a sighting of thick ankles, a trademark of the women down the generations of family, through a sea of legs and feet. A recognition. Doesn't matter where this happens, far from home; the distance is probably what makes it work, what makes it potent.

I am in a Russian bar in New York City, the *Russian Samovar,* listening to a poetry recital. Because I arrived late I am trapped on the staircase up to the performance space. I can only glimpse the poet's face but hear clearly his words as I sit on the edge of the room at the level of all of the legs positioned under tables. Here is a pair of legs enclosed in school-supply grey stockings with ankles that are solid, as impressive as a horse's fetlocks. They take me back to home, to Perth and the site of family. When I was a girl I was appalled at the idea that I would follow into this monstrosity at their age: that my legs would grow into horse's legs. The formidable line of sisters, my grandmother's sisters. Except they were never in a line by the time I was born: they fought each other constantly over half a century and formed alliances of two each time they needed to. At shin level in a room of strangers in this sophisticated gathering where words are the most highly valued commodity, I concentrate on such legacies. This is the start of my desire to make a picture of family, skeins and threads of specific lives, of people, of the myths used to tell its stories. A flood of remembering follows.

Will I remove the flesh and blood, banish bodies so as not to embarrass anyone? Show only the lines and paths that are left, a decommissioned living: traces, crystalline threads on the edges of former body occupation? You can't be too careful, the older relatives declare to me, one after the other.

I am in my home town — Perth, Western Australia. A landscape marked out with harm. I have grown up with stories full of dramatic moments. The more dramatic usually means more laden with harm. This informs the map I use to get around, and allows me to recall, without any prompting, what happened on that corner; in that arcade, one floor up. Suburbs share the burdens that the city once shouldered by its centrality. In this hotel, downstairs from where I sit, a couple of weeks ago a man cut his lover, cut his throat right across. A lovers' tiff, a Saturday night, a dishonouring description, nothing like any argument I have ever had. In a public place, this gay bar in the city. I don't know if their coupling was over, finished before the fateful night. A small ocean of red; police, ambulance; the end of the night someone was sober. He survived, just, is what I heard.

The history is here for all of us to live up to. A history of horrors, and in the middle of all of this we move along, making anew and staying away from fear. I stay here willingly, and mark out the streets with landmarks and knowledge of what happened once upon a time, imprinted too with what now happens to me.

locations

I was born in 1959. That was the year my father played in the Grand Final of the Australian Rules code for the Subiaco Football Club, a club which hadn't managed to win a premiership since 1924, the sentimental underdogs.

The men are in high spirits. They won their match today and there is a bonus coming their way: that was the promise earlier in the season. Young men on the make, they have trained hard all season and now it is paying off. Something so satisfying about the really hard games: the rubbing down in the change rooms; the cold out there and then the steamy showers and clean bodies smelling of Deep Heat; and the bonhomie of victory. And the anticipation of a few drinks and probably sex tonight, at least some hot and heavy petting. The men are at their peak, the girls who follow them young and sometimes innocent, but worth the wait. None of these men has his own house to live in; they all board in rooms and bringing a girl home for many of them is out of the question. Most of the time the sex happens in the back seat of their cars, or out the back of the Leederville Town Hall or the other halls which have regular dances.

The supporters of the team, Subiaco, are ecstatic; many of them have waited too much of their adult lives for this culmination of the dedicated effort of consistent training and good form. 1959 might just be the year. The problem with men at their peak of athletic skill is that they are also often keen on erotic adventures, and desired by young women. And erotic adventure so often takes with it the tastes of alcohol, late nights, other indulgences. Certainly distractions, a lack of concentration on the field. There is so much invested in this season that all of them are jumpy.

I was there in 1973 to watch them finally triumphant, breaking the most dismal record of all. By this time I was a teenager; it was years since my father's football career had finished. He had already begun to reminisce about the football years, a period of ten years or so into his late twenties when the men would tear through the game in order to start the party. For years, this conception of *family* was my model and I had little need for blood relations. We attended every game of the season and I played on the oval after matches; investigating the boxes of match programs and other things deemed worthy of keeping under tables in dank clubrooms. Following that combination of a rich mentholated smell and the high odour of male bodies, peeking into change rooms later while it was still pungent. We all lived together, too, the players and their wives and fledgling families, in a new housing estate with regulation houses.

At some time unmarked by incident the focus changed. And now, I yearn to be part of a longer story of blood and connection. Perhaps this is what happens when you don't have children of your own to keep the line flowing; perhaps it is an act of compensation, this recording.

~

Old Jesse E Hammond decided to make a gift to his home town as the new century commenced. He drew a plan of Perth from memory, back in time to the years 1871–2. I don't know why he chose those years. He seemed to have an excellent knowledge of the thirty or so streets he filled in with merchants and residences and public buildings. Did other people help him, or did he make the map alone? Was it a reverie at the end of his life? I would love to know whom he consulted, or the range of aides-mémoires he applied to make this map. Those famous names of the Six Hungry Families of Perth[4] are well represented and haven't changed much in all of these years.

Up north on the map, near to where I live, is a *Two roomed cottage built in 12 hours by D. Gray*; it's just around the corner from *Love Lane.* Nobody lived or traded in *Love Lane.*

mythopoeia

This is a story of female fertility. A mythopoeia.

Ideas of new beginnings, of a new world, implicit in the movement from England to Western Australia. The appalling results: they are the legacy of not passing on stories. I'm telling other people's stories because nobody else has. Or ever will.

I tell family secrets, benign secrets now, they can't do any harm. Secrets about death and loss and sufferings.

The voice in his belly told Theodore Krakouer to destroy the world. With words, too, simply by using them, I am destroying, smashing up, the world of the family. I don't mean to do anyone any harm.

searching for meaning: Julie

I have been dreaming of Julie for months. She comes back and tells me that she should have come to Perth to talk to us about what she was fearful of. She has missed her mother's funeral and getting to know all the nieces and nephews born since her death. She didn't have time to say goodbye to anyone.

There is a pall of silence hanging over our family. It holds Julie.

This time is as good as any to open the vaults of the family; to lay its secrets bare, and prepare for the necessary scrutiny. Except the word *vault* is too grand: there are only scraps of barely remembered detail. We live in a time that invites attentiveness to the past, acts of exorcism or fascination. Or connection: a desire for a tangible lineage and not just the expurgated versions. Even when we are together as an extended family, three generations of us, there is a fracture of purpose, an unease that we seem to have been carrying with us all our lives. Too much unspoken holds each of us back. I look at the family gathered on the night of Christmas, and later in the photograph albums we insist upon, and I see this longing in every one of us to speak, to let go of the burden of silence we carry. Perhaps to talk about Julie.

The family line shows in our faces, features passed along the generations. A little collection of distinction: wide ankles and laugh lines. The voices of the family are bleatings, holding little coherence.

You are not present here: you have gone. What we have left are photographs and memories of the pleasurable parts of childhoods we were just leaving.

Nobody will be injured by any of this candour, not now. This impulse is about challenging the convenient myths that we have inherited and, in good faith, perpetuated. It is charged with thinking about the way forward.

My cousin died when she concealed a pregnancy twenty years ago. To write of the disaster of her death is still dangerous. To apprehend the disaster cannot return her, but perhaps it can restore some dignity to her memory. She died without the right of reply.

I am compelled to imagine for you. Were the moments before loss of consciousness, predictable as Hollywood, filled with a slide show of the progress of your life? Two weeks away from a birthday and you considered whether the gifts would be better selected this year. Your family was good at getting it wrong, but often only just: a tiny amount more either of money or planning and you could have been happy with what was given.

Remembering, panicky and out-of-control. Remembering senses more than experiences: swimming in pools in childhood, learning to drive, seeing blood. Riding your cousin's pony at twelve through a lush field near a river, an unknown place, feeling a ripple pass over your skin when you listened to music you liked.

This dull pain of the last weeks, a shifting of hemispheres. You haven't known what to do about it, so have held it in abeyance. Why didn't anyone notice, why didn't they say anything to you? You now recognise your own responses: you had not acted until whatever was wrong was noticed by someone else. Nobody did. What does this make you?

You deliberately kept it at a great distance from yourself.

It is her body, her life. What a remarkable way for it to end, in this explosion of pain, a big bubble of blood that suddenly bursts; a taste of iron in her mouth, the sense of emergency as the light leaves her vision. Alone.

I want to try to understand something: how a young woman could die in the way Julie did. Her friends often guarded her like hawks and wouldn't let her talk to strangers. What would happen if she did? No one can tell yet that Julie is carrying a child because she has hidden it so well for all of these months.

We grew up in the same time and place: that is our link, both starting our lives as children in working-class families. That might be one of the causes of her premature death: moving up and into an imagined middle class. Not as easy as it might seem; involving delicate negotiations and codes.

It's true. We thought we were part of a classless Australia.

That is what we had been told. Egalitarian: a fair-minded nation that started off as a penal colony. We thought we had membership, had joined the club. We had friends who were millionaires! Perth was like that; it was changing fast. There was money to be made, fame to be earned. A film, a drama about the latest boom time, called *The Nickel Queen,* was made in Perth, and locals, if they were lucky, could be part of the crowd scenes. But you had to also mind your step; you could be pulled down if you crossed over the line.

I have always thought that she was a few years younger than I was, but she was born in the following year, in 1960. My mother took her home from the hospital and she lived with us for her first few weeks because her own mother had three babies already, each with the minimum time for conception between them. Her mother had her five babies in five-and-a-half years.

The decade of the 1970s, her only decade as an adult, was such an odd time to grow up in Australia: full of flux and swirling patterns, in politics and economics and social life. I'm convinced now that I was unaware of the borders separating class and of where I belonged — not understood until much later, after my private, single-sex school education, and my entry into university. Nobody else in my family, on either side, had ever finished school and continued into higher education. Perhaps you cannot know such things until you have made the shifts, commenced your own life. What does *working class* mean, anyway?

Most of my friends have *transcended* their working-class roots: that is, at least, what we say when we talk about ourselves over dinner in stylish restaurants, those earnest markers of our mobility.

How did I comprehend this disaster: Julie's surprising death? And how can I reconcile myself to it now?

lovers and best friends

Him. Ghosts from earlier years cram in and keep me free from loneliness. It has been nearly twenty years since I met him and fell in love and then out of love.

Half of my life so far. I can't recall his features well enough to know if that figure I've seen now for three days is him: a pathetic cliché of loneliness, living mostly on the streets, unable to keep clean. Is it him, my once-precious beloved body, my first lover? He may still be safe and sound in the family home, protected into his fifth decade from the cruelty of the world, buffered in a space without judgement or responsibility. An infantile space. In his family, cosseted by their abiding faith.

Her. The day is overcast but filled with the promise of Perth summers-to-come when we make a pact of friendship that will last for the next twenty years. Three decades: seventies, eighties, nineties, and then it will be over. What we do that day is escape study, escape the partying that begins on the last day of semester and swirls around our familiar haunts and even the quiet corners, and we go off together, alone. We drive to the beach and we immerse ourselves in sea water and sand, fully clothed; we sit and talk and consolidate our affection and the knowledge we have so far of each other. She reads me the letter that a teacher has just given her, accompanying her final assessment; we sit in a mock sort of stupor. The letter is a coded love letter: his fantasies about a beautiful young woman, full of promise and without a full awareness yet of the currents of power and allure she can generate. It is a sad little letter; I've written my own versions in the years that follow: attempting one thing with another and making a declaration of utter obscurity. Desiring the direct approach: saying *I want to fuck you* or *I adore you*. Instead writing a fable about writing and artifice and life. She told me on the beach that day she was still a virgin. Sex was unthinkable with a man as old as her father, *not for her first time* anyway.

We learnt so much about each other that day, as much as we likely did over all the years that followed. Told special secrets about our families, our shame, and, I suppose, something approximating our ambition, which was not an idea we consciously toyed with at our age and in our time. The malaise that followed sitting my final school exams and just passing, during the weeks when the Whitlam government was dismissed and another election called, made me not at all ambitious anyway, even if I was unable to name what I felt. We were confused: both of us were the first ever in our families to be admitted to higher education and we weren't sure of the codes. Terrified of being caught out by either side: the ruling class or militant fellow students who seemed to know what they were talking about. Ambition — a profoundly bourgeois concept. As our façade, or pretence, was solidly bourgeois in our first year at university, we were obliged to avoid it through rebellion. I am still confused. Skeletons rattled in the closet where our "working" class was hidden. The best thing I can say is that we learned about effective concealment.

Our first meeting was auspicious and set the tone for

our future together, one that lasted longer than any marriage we'll have. I'm thinking of her now, and she enters my narrative because she was my house mate when Julie died. She was the one I came home to after the funeral. Our young lives were smouldering; sex had begun for both of us; so, in an official sense, had our adulthood.

These two became a new version of family, an ersatz family for me.

girls together

But let me go back to the beginning of the decade, and to Julie. We were girls together in our school holidays. Holiday time spent with the cousins in the country in the 1970s, in a small town of contrasts: Plymouth Brethren; farmers; boys in black jeans, already with large chips on their shoulders. Being from the city gave me the advantage of sophistication.

Staying in a house in town with an aunt and uncle and their children. A mother, a father who is always at work, and seven children. All of us are girls bar one, all in the tight age range of five years. The girls near to my age have made me smuggle three special pairs of new sandals my mother has just bought for school and for good and forbidden me to take to the country. Red, white and navy blue. The same style. They satisfy all of us for the two weeks. We wear them every day, walking into town to the milk bar and out into the bush. We have ruined them by the time they are packed for home.

The landscape we drive across is flat, with only the narrowest gradations of difference. None of the towns we drive through appeals to me, and the drive, every single time, seems longer than it should be. All of that anticipation of being together, being away from home, wearing those brand new sandals. Then too, there are mysteries about girlhood to which I seek answers from my cousins. They are about concerns I would never speak of explicitly, because I don't know the questions yet and, most importantly, because I am too shy to risk revealing things. As an adult, I repeat this behaviour, over and again; I name it to myself as the result of ironic distance, but others receive it as a truth. A lover, once, later in my life, swore that on our first night together I described as *down there* the place I wanted to be touched. I couldn't believe, or remember, such coyness in the heat of that lust.

Our grandmother comes with us for half of the holiday this year. We aim to be free of her as early as we can every day. We make our way to the bitumen square of the drive-in theatre and find enough in the droppings from the nights before and the funny shapes of spinifex in the lawn, the big painted screen, and the boxed carriers of movie sound, to keep us there for half the day. Grim pickings, with none of the allure of the starlit evenings. Sometimes we are allowed to sit in the family car, driven around there after tea, teenagers together without adult supervision. Preparing for the drama of love and sex in our near future, imagining what it will be like, feeling wildly impatient that we are still children, we practise kissing on our own arms. Doing this in the bleak landscape of the drive-in lot, and the repressive one of a world where we know that nothing can happen until we are first married: people can be hounded out of town after adultery and separation. We know nothing about what it is like after violence in the home, but we are sure we know, by heart, every act perpetrated at the height of the passion of betrayal. With our active imaginations, we are all convinced we will someday be brides and then mothers, married ladies who can go down to the shops and expect respect. It is an idea gleaned from our own mothers and how they carry themselves; I don't think we contemplated them as models; we were too close to them.

We watch Telethon all night on TVW 7. About ten of us; girls in our middle teenage years and some smaller children we are babysitting. Telethon was the highlight of Perth's entertainment and civic-minded life each year: for twenty-four hours the provincial television station charitably quits normal programming to raise money for medical research into childhood illnesses. The reward for donations is entertainment, more akin to the bawdy music hall than television, and the opportunity to prove once again that, despite its small population, Perth people are the most generous of all Australians. Singers and comedians and television actors are flown to Perth to offer annual glamour, and we are to realise just how many talented people also live in Perth: newsreaders, gardening experts, singers and comedians, women with huge breasts that just fit into a bikini for the camera. In the face of the suffering of others, especially the little kiddies and their poor parents, we can be proud of ourselves, the generous people of Perth. Always a striptease after midnight, mimed singing and dancing, a sexual frisson between locals and stars on-screen. White faces painted black. Something is not-quite-right for many of these participants. Many bodies are needed to fill the late slots in those twenty-four hours, so quality control is lax.

Julie

One of our country-town holidays happened when I was thirteen. That year, we three eldest girls are together long enough to influence our menstrual cycles, which fall into line. We sleep together in a double bed and marvel at our biology. Six years later and Julie is dead. Before she turned nineteen, she died. Close in age to Ena, our grandmother, when she gave birth to her first child, an illegitimate girl. Julie *fell* into pregnancy in the small country town she lived in. She felt the shame of this keenly: I know this, not because she had the chance to tell me, but because of her actions. She told no one, perhaps she even kept it from herself, went without medical supervision and proper nutrition, and continued to wear her tight black jeans.

She killed herself, but it was a subtle suicide: the foetus died at an advanced stage and her body was poisoned with septicaemia. The doctor described it as gangrene. I don't know why there was this imprecision of diagnosis; perhaps it was because "gangrene" was more consolingly specific, a concept easier for the family to understand.

It was too late; she died in the flurry of emergency. Not for her the ignominy of a botched abortion attempt, or the struggle of single motherhood. She held her secret within her body, enclosed it, as tight and fearfully as you can imagine. She died from the shame. Who was she afraid of? She "fell" into the line of transgressors in the family, women who had sex and became pregnant outside of marriage — secretly.

him

The pious boy remains locked into the romance of the Catholic Church as an adult man. So close to agnosticism that I would have claimed it for him on our first date, but he tells me that he adores the new Pope, the one from Poland, John Paul the Second. He buys a remaindered book of his poems about human love, published before his elevation to the papal throne, on our second date, spending his last four dollars that couldn't really be spared. I paid for coffee and the drinks at the pub. By the time we are living together, his father has died before his time, just after retirement. We attend the funeral together as a couple. I have a place in the family because I am a sensible young woman. Living in sin is my only fault. This is my first Catholic funeral, and I am shocked by the numerous claims of guilty secrets and hellish punishments. The father had lived a moderate life but perhaps the priest knows something we don't. It is a bad time to introduce such uncertainty into our lives, I thought, as a novice to Catholicism.

Another funeral, years before my boyfriend's father's. Julie, my sweet-natured cousin. We weren't religious in our extended family, but if we had been, I don't know how her death could have been explained. I suspect it would have been concealed, masked over, just as it was in our agnosticism.

her

We remained as best friends for decades. She had a talent and a taste for pop stars and invested heavily in her pastime. She got involved with two of the men from one band that was the biggest thing to happen in Australian pop music since the *Easybeats*. This meant superior hotel rooms and hire cars and fancy drinks backstage, and, while they were not necessarily fashionable in the circles she aspired to, her achievements were not insignificant. Although she could tell only some of her friends of her conquests, just her closest friends, all the details were fairly spectacular. I was more modest about whom I chose to have sex with. It hadn't really happened yet. At the same time as Julie was poisoning herself, I was responsibly attending a family planning clinic for the Pill. I had tried to do it before and got lost driving in circles looking for the clinic. In the heat of Perth's summer, my first urine sample seemed to cloud up before my eyes and after thirty minutes of driving I gave up, secretly pleased that I wouldn't have to go through the interview and answer those questions. I was taking precautions before I needed to; I was still a virgin, but hopeful.

When I was eleven I had a boyfriend. This was when we lived in a town with not enough young single women, where the Malay and Japanese pearl divers and labourers were sentenced to an odd celibate life. That is, I think, why he came after me. But didn't I, too, go after him? I was innocent and I met him at the beach after school with my horse and my friend with her horse. She was older; her boyfriend also Malay. They got caught and I think he was flogged or run out of town. I learnt how to kiss with my gentle grown-up man who touched me with great modesty on my breasts. Who also touched my tummy but no further. I can still remember his smell: baby powder and grown-up musky. Nicer than any other man I have smelled.

I'm shocked to remember this and how young I was. Until other rivalries in the schoolyard surfaced, when some girls were overlooked and others chosen, this pre-pubescent carnival ran smoothly. Once the anonymous letters were circulated to headmasters and parents, there was hell to pay.

When we were children we were told cautionary tales about sex and its results, and mostly they were so wrong-headed that they resulted only in confusion and fear. As an adult there is the luxury of looking back on this and finding it to be nonsense and amusing, but this is too generous. They told us, and some of us believed it, that girls became sick because they fell through the bonnets of cars belonging to fast boys. Once, a snakebite forced a girl into hospital in another city for many months and when she came back she was quite changed.

When I finally walked out of a family planning clinic with a prescription for birth control pills I felt like a grown-up. But it was quite some time before I needed the pharmaceutical protection. One of the differences between Julie and I was that I lived in the city and she didn't. I had access to these confidential health services. Women in small communities often needed to arrange a trip to the city or another town if they wanted to avoid being crunched in the gossip mill. For us, in Perth, sex was so easy, after the first time.

Julie

I am wild with fury. I don't believe how silent we have been for these decades.
Julie.
Julie.
Julie.
You died because you didn't want to admit you were pregnant?

Since then I've met women who set up women's health services in Perth during the 1970s. Working harder than they imagined against a harsh morality that punished people with the repercussions of "bad" behaviour, and which refused to let people take responsibility for themselves, including their mistakes. This was politics: these women spoke the unspeakable, and they learnt so much about things like bureaucratic structures and health models and leasing premises and the differences *between* people that later many of them became senior executives in government and commerce, leaders in the community.

There were women who gave up all manner of the comforts they already had for political beliefs; they gave up parts of their lives for the feminism they had absorbed into themselves. They told each other stories. For many of them it was the thing that can happen when *suddenly* your eyes are opened and you see clearly all of those cloudy ambiguities and then that single line that shows you how all of the rest is skewed. *Ah, heterosexual presumption. Ah, racism. Sexism.* And spoke out in ways they hadn't before. Caused scandals. Much of it was hushed up. These were times when sex was still considered and named as *naughty*, when sex was dirty, men's business, and rape was barely spoken of, despite its investiture in the Criminal Code.

I was a teenager then, and I heard some of these rumblings. I was nervous — maybe I still am — about what happens after the acquisition of such knowledge, and of how destructive family life can be. How a terrifying pathology can be carried through the lineage of a family. So much happened from the start to the end of that decade, and still my cousin died.

Julie, why couldn't you talk? If I can, I don't understand why you were so silent. Afraid of what? I don't want you dead and us silent.

Consciousness-raising and women's clinics didn't happen in country towns like Dalwallinu, Dowerin, Narrogin, Northam. Not even when mothers and sisters and aunts and friends were starting to liberate themselves about sex, and some of them *lived in sin*. We still didn't talk about it. This was such a straitlaced and silencing society. Now, worldly-wise, used to talking about anything, I'm surprised to remember those regulations.[5]

The social upheavals of the 1960s did not really happen in Perth until the next decade. Still, a prevailing myth about this place is that it *lost its innocence* in 1963 when a mass murderer began to shoot people through open windows, to enter flats that were unlocked, to take shots at young lovers in cars. After this time, our doors had to be locked and *we grew up*. Perth became a dangerous place and everybody had a mass murderer story.[6] As if the sea of alcohol and its effects in the streets of Perth in the 1850s constituted the innocence of the past.

We grew up, all of the girls I knew, expecting to marry and have children. That was the minimum requirement. Julie and I are the only girls in my extended family who won't marry, the only two who didn't have a baby. Some of the cousins have already married twice. Why was Julie silent? If she had known how common it was to get pregnant, would it have been different?

him

I see him again suddenly on a Friday night, my Catholic lover. This is ten years after we split up — the beginning of the 1990s, in my golden age. I am feeling invincible and happy, in a time when I am being accorded what I consider special considerations, spoiled with particular privileges. My highly esteemed days. I am driving to a concert I have been invited to. It is a Friday night so there are people on the streets, even in St George's Terrace, despite its lack of any retail trade. Waiting at the lights on the short drive to the Concert Hall, I turn around at precisely the moment he comes into view in the foyer area of the Reserve Bank building, all lit up for the cleaning staff. He is methodical, making himself busy, half a street away from me. He can't see me. I am sealed and protected in the body of my little car, feeling as though I am looking back onto the past, and I am. He was my lover, my partner in another life, a precious liability I managed to discard. We might have had a baby together, once, and be still connected in some arrangement of access to or custody of a now teenaged child. But I had managed to escape that and make a life of my own, which was now full of the kind of riches that he always valued. Before I saw him, I was on top of the world. This was a body left behind. Not nostalgic, not regretful. Just intrigued, with that luxury of being separate.

The weakness that sings through my body: he terrorised me and I stayed. Why did I stay? What was it that kept me with him? The last time we had met was years ago, when he was so full of shallow bravado and deep hubris that he still served as a danger to me. It happened on the morning after the first night with a new lover, my first since him. I was radiant in the way that sex can make you, and was able for the first time to deflect with ease everything he had to give. It was the most powerful moment in all the years we had known each other, putting paid to my shame.

Yes, it was him those years later working late into each Friday night as a cleaner. I found myself taking that route through the city just to check, to see him from a distance. I kept it up for a year or so.

Julie

Julie is quiet, always has been. Self-absorbed and thoughtful. Resourceful, but she will never dazzle: hers is a slow burn, a satisfaction-in-the-getting-there. Look at her photographs as a young teenager; don't forget that she was dead before she finished her teens. She looks halfway between a boy and a girl, pretty but with an absence of the girlish flourishes that we, sisters and cousins, flaunted. We played around with colours and style; we displayed ourselves all of the time; we learnt about feminine wiles and gathered beauty tips. We even went to deportment and modelling classes at the Julie McFarlane Modelling Academy in Barrack Street, under the tutelage of the legendary Marjory McGann.

I think Julie would have been a wonderful and generous lover, full of affection and patience. She was the spirited one in all of our gatherings: not with exuberance but with genuine interest and care. She took her lover's identity with her, secreted it away; in death she protected him. Told nobody. I hope he deserved it; hope he was a lover and not a man who forced himself into her.

There were all those months, nearly nine months, of having a foetus growing inside her. A time when some women grow comfortable with their bodies for the first time, read it as a remarkable living extension of themselves, less abstract than ever before. The pain is, for once, productive. The girl had all these changes in her body; she kept quiet about all of them. She pretended that they weren't happening.

This act of violence. Her denial. Submerged, and she didn't fight back, she didn't ask anyone for help. I hope she didn't. It is easier to imagine the disaster as being of her making.

At the funeral, was our grandmother Ena thinking about her own similar experience in 1929? Did she think about her secret? Because it was still her own secret at that time; she had held it close and told no one, certainly none of her children. It was revealed much later. When Julie died, Ena's own illegitimate baby was turning fifty. Another silent transgressor. Her baby was born when she wasn't married or properly prepared to be a mother. Fifty years later, she was at this funeral, the burying of her grand daughter, and nobody knew what had happened to her. I plunder my memory of that day, that terrible funeral, for evidence of how my grandmother behaved, for any slippages: of recognition, of a return to her own pain. I find nothing definitive.

In each generation of our Australian family there has been shame about a pregnancy. How is it that Julie paid the highest price, in 1978, in the fifth generation? There is a gap in the family now: her place. Julie's.

I wish I could show you a photograph of her. When she had slightly buck teeth and scraggly hair but was still quite beautiful. Half-boy and half-girl. The person she most reminded me of — all of us saw this resemblance — was Brigitte Bardot, without her buxom chest.

She was buried in one of those cemeteries in country town Australia, rich and green and respectfully tended in some sections, a bit messier in others. I don't think this horticulture was a split down religious lines, but I could be wrong. We travelled from Perth for three hours in a fast and comfortable car to get there. We drove in silence, in mute horror and dread at what might happen. That was separate from our grief.

Our grandfather, who had always wanted to be burned or tossed out with the rubbish, unconcerned about his body's next phase, became sentimental and fearful as he was dying of throat cancer and insisted then that he wanted to be peacefully buried, not burned. *I've suffered enough*, he told his family.

All of these people on display, required to enable the ritual to happen.

Grave diggers on duty.

We must stand out here in the open. It is the middle of winter and it has been raining all day. Our path is slippery; the ground around the hole where we are standing is muddy. But this isn't why the women in the family — mother and sisters to the dead girl — all slide toward the big shiny coffin. That is grief, solidarity towards her. Each needs to be restrained by someone stronger, in each case a man; for a while it looked dangerous.

Ena is here, standing with me.

Looking back at this terrible day, I don't recall that there was a service, just the movement between a sister's house and the cemetery and back again before the silent drive home. I don't know what I was thinking. It was a time when I was first living away from home, my first shared house. The first house mate, my best friend who had encouraged us to make the move out of home together, would give her notice to me within weeks. We had lasted only a few weeks, anyway; her boyfriend talked her into moving in with him. She was my best friend; it was the first of her minor betrayals, enacted with a flourish and her characteristic attention to maximising conflict. Later, when we are mature women, she consults a fortune teller who tells her she is impeded by her unresolved conflict with her mother. She decides that I am her mother and she rejects me, but without any explanation. For weeks I blunder along and don't even realise that she isn't returning my telephone calls. Then come the notes telling me there is something wrong but cannot yet be discussed. It is only after she has betrayed other friends that I hear about the fortune-teller.

You are being buried in the ground and we are here to witness it.
Your full family.
This is my first funeral.
This little town might have something to do with your death.

It has taken us hours to travel here; it is a nightmare.
I cannot imagine your silence over those months.

The people clever enough to have taken tranquillisers handed out earlier are now much calmer. It has quietened them; it makes your burial possible.

Where do we go from here?

me

In times of distress, the body can be both the first and the last thing to go. Minor symptoms, daily, remind you of your predicament. Little smells that are quite unfamiliar, discharges, and pains that cannot be adequately described, so you just go on living with them. And then, some way down the track, it might take another forty years, smooth workings finish finally, abruptly.

Julie must have considered her symptoms: the swelling in the abdomen, the end of the problem of disposing of menstrual blood, the feeling of having a parasite in her body. Perhaps she absorbed them as natural and didn't question where they would take her. Didn't she take sex education classes at school? Personal hygiene, liberal Sunday School lessons, human biology? Don't tell me they weren't part of the curriculum in her neck of the woods.

When I was a teenager my father, in a paralysis of grief after loss, began to grow an appendix to his belly button. It was like an intact body coming out to face us; it kept growing right through winter. We were alarmed at first, and then began to treat it affectionately, with some humour and less disgust than we would now. My father refused to see a doctor, despite our fears of the thing invading the house while we slept. This was before even the first of the *Alien* films had been made, but we knew the general principle of dangerous bodily invasions.

Instead, he took the matter into his own hands, with our assistance. My little sister donated her tiny orthodontic rubber bands, like ponytail bands for dolls, and we fastened one to the middle of the beast in an attempt to stunt its growth. It took some weeks, but it worked: the thick fleshy thing shrivelled up and never grew back. It seemed to retreat back into his body: there was no detachment, no evidence. As an adult, I contend that the growth was his body offering up a resistance to his grief. This abject addition to the life of the family was handled with equanimity by his daughters.

And then there is Julie's emergency, her parasite also finally exposed to the scrutiny of the outside world. I keep asking my friend who trained in obstetrics and in emergency medicine what would have happened, and he keeps deflecting my question.

official stories

A final item to gather up after thinking about Julie for so long, about this family, takes me back to the office of the State's Registrar-General, the keeper of Births and Deaths and Marriages, an office regularly crowded by sorrow, where people come to find out who they are. Sounds ridiculous, but that thread of blood, that certainty about lineage, might be accompanied by reasons for having endured such an awful life, that it can all be explained as outside your control. The hope of that means a great deal to many people in their search for meanings. In this office, where they play loud rock-and-roll music to drown out most noises, people cluster and are sometimes rewarded with the full picture:

Father
Mother
Witnesses
Conjugal Condition of Deceased
Disposal of Body

Once when I was lurking in the tenth floor office of the Registrar-General, I met a young Aboriginal boy from Halls Creek who had spent the night on the bus to get there. His first visit to Perth and here he was, looking for details of his birth, of his parents, clues for his adulthood. They couldn't find him in their book of lists; he had the spellings wrong. More work was needed to find out where he fitted in.

I have taken my time to order Julie's death certificate. Full of trepidation on the nights before I could pick it up, I wondered how detailed it would be. Three working days to take delivery and twenty-seven dollars for a full extract. It didn't tell me, of course, how long she had known she was *with child.* At first glance I was disappointed:

> Death subject of coronial inquiry.
> Notification of cause of death not
> received at date of registration.

I run back in and ask: *how do I find out the results of the coronial inquiry?*

I am told: *look on the right hand margin.* And there it is:

MEMORANDUM
The entry in column 4(1) is now replaced by the required particulars as follow:-
Cerebral haemorrhage due to toxaemia of pregnancy.
(As determined at Northam on 22 August 1978 by C. Zempilas, Coroner.)

The pure silence around that girl and her baby. Folding into itself. A grief without a voice.

hardships

A fear, a fantasy.

You walk innocently into this dank outhouse, the public conveniences. Ladies' toilets and washrooms in a park somewhere, or a beachside complex, or even those sets of cleaner, antiseptic-smelling toilets in a shopping mall in the city, or a department store. The ones that used to have attendants on duty, to clean up after you. Walk into the cubicle, eager to empty your bladder, it's been a while since you realised you needed this, a time taken to locate this convenience. This is a place for quick business, no sitting and thinking — straight in and out, for relief only. And what lies there in the bowl elicits a response that floats between horror and your deepest compassion. A body, a tiny red thing, a baby, recently delivered, in here, the blood of its birth all over. A red flesh thing wedged in the bowl. Alive or not? This is your chance to prove something to yourself, that you are brave, a brave and adult woman. You must pull it out and see if you can revive it, to at least see whether it is dead or not. What trauma has this little body just endured? What about its mother?

The little body is smeared with vernix; there is still stuff in its mouth; the umbilical cord lying there like a fat plait. There is some stirring, some sign of life; I fear blood, a lifelong squeamishness, I hesitate before I follow the steps for mouth-to-mouth. I'm surprised that it's a split-second decision. It's made; I do it; it's alive. Only now am I aware of the blood trail out of the cubicle, out of the main door, the way I am running to find help, to keep this mess in my arms alive.[7]

White City: Ena Krakouer Le Comte

The grand daughter develops a need to picture the family, and begins to compile a version of it out of nothing: reaching towards the desired object is my yearning. I find nothing. Then gradually little paths to information open out, paths to a midden laden with other lives, those who shared a world with these forebears. I find bits and pieces: tantalising scandals and what sound like plaintive cries for help or for an end to this investigation. Sometimes written in someone's hand.

Often it isn't possible for decades anyway for such a need to be satisfied. Usually it comes through education or the accumulation of money: the desire to remake a family with words and an attention to select lines of history. This is the moment when I begin to constitute a thing called my family. Before, except at funerals and the occasional wedding, we are a set of individuals, without a larger framework of belonging. And afterwards, when I have made this framework I name *Krakouer*, will there be cohesion? I doubt it. What is more likely is debris left over from a set of explosions.

Start with the photograph taken at the end of the nineteenth century. I claim to be a descendant of the people posed on the verandah. That is not hard as I met three of them during their long lives. This looks like a Sunday afternoon, after lunch. Children, parents, grandparents: all the adults in couples. The four children belong to my great-grandparents, David and Jessie Krakouer, including their baby Abe, named after his notorious uncle, on his mother's lap. My grandmother Ena will not be born for ten years. There is another small boy who poses alongside his tricycle. Somebody, an earlier family historian, has written the names of the Krakouers in the photograph in ballpoint onto their bodies: they are marked in this way for the benefit of future family. The other people are not identified, though it is clear through family resemblance and common sense that they are Jessie's family. Her parents look formidable; her siblings look like her. She has delicate little plaits that swirl into a bun, and she has a strong-featured face. Her husband is handsome and looks confident. He leans out to the side of the verandah with one arm, as though holding it up, and his other hand rests on his hip. The men all have a corsage on their lapels. The people are well dressed, there are ornate cane chairs with printed cushions, camellias bloom to one side of the photograph.

My head holds these dead people. I have fallen unwittingly into a pastime about which I am sceptical. I see people in libraries and archives and Family History Centres, obsessed with finding traces of family in microform, in scraps of paper, officially, and sometimes arbitrarily, preserved for posterity. Going blind, forgetting about their own lives, learning to love a different intensity of light in this search for clues. The linkages we make with strangers, through blood.

In the Mormon Family History Centre in an unlikely suburb of Perth, the woman counselled me before she helped me to look through the archives of nineteenth-century lives. *Even if a child dies at birth, even if it never becomes an infant, it is still a member of that family. It is still a loss, a sadness, a little name and memory. Dear, you must always respect these losses.*

Selectively, I choose the three sisters I am most interested in and I follow some of the progress of their lives. I find out as much as I can about them.

Ena

My grandmother died at a bingo table, in the middle of a game. Her friends turned to her because she was uncharacteristically quiet, and when one of them touched her arm she fell off her chair and was pronounced dead when the ambulance arrived at the hospital. She died doing one of the things she loved. It was all so quick, the pain at the end of life not an enduring one; she didn't drag everyone down with her.

The first image recalled of the grandmother's house also holds a smell: that of regular cooking. Roasted meats and vegetables, and the fat that enables a thorough browning. The storage of smells from decades of family meals in a small kitchen of a small house, the cooking residue seeping into the walls. In some ways it is a comforting welcome to the children spending their weekends and school holidays with Nana.

In its heyday as the family home, this little house had held seven people. More often than not, though, there were even more adult bodies present during these years because the parents were social creatures. Children were born between 1937 and 1949: three girls and then two boys.

Years later, after the death of my grandmother, the last person living there, the house is sold and then renovated. In a short time the new industrious owner becomes a minor media celebrity after exposing less-than-scrupulous procedures in monitoring blood donations at the beginning of the AIDS epidemic. He is both haemophilic and now HIV-positive, and in his grief becomes militant. Every time he is interviewed for television he is standing at the front of my grandmother's old house. Where once there was lawn there is now a cottage garden; where once there was an illustration of Mighty Mouse on the eaves, drawn and coloured during the 1960s by one of the adolescent sons, now there is lattice directing the growth of jasmine. Each time the family sees the house on the television, all those remaining, they think about land values, improvements and their own lost opportunities.

Thinking in the aftermath of a life takes me right back to when it was first built; moving into it, in 1938, with their first baby already arrived to make them properly a family. And beyond that event, before, to the young people the mother and father had once been. And then a sharp jolt into the impossibility of taking this anywhere: there is nobody to ask the questions about Ena as a girl and young woman. Every memory is now affected by her death, by mistakes she made during her life, by her lapses of judgement, her tenderness, her humour.

On the second day of June, 1929, when Ena Krakouer gave birth to a daughter she named Beryl Merle at Hillcrest Hospital in Harvest Road, Fremantle, she was alone and nineteen years old. She is listed as the informant as well as the mother on the birth certificate, and the witnesses to the birth were all employees of Hillcrest, a midwife-nurse and another woman who may have been a domestic or nurse.

Nobody in her family, aside from her sisters and mother and a cousin, who all kept utterly silent, knew about this baby until 1980 when the baby, all grown up, arrived at her sister's doorstep, the year after her mother Ena died. Ena took her secret to her grave, as they say. Soon after, the family had to be reshaped, to be extended to take in one more child. The span of Ena's child-bearing years stretched out to twenty.

It is almost impossible to imagine Ena as a young woman when I only knew her as a grandmother. Impossible after the discovery of her secret child. I knew her as a cheery, social woman, but that's all. When Ena married Paul Raoul Le Comte in 1935, both of them already had a child and both had left that child in the care of others. They could be described as being *experienced* in the world. Ena waited for eight years, until 1937, before she had another baby, waited until she was a married lady. In 1977, when I drove her to a doctor's appointment and sat in on the consultation, I realised the extent of her neglect of her body, her hard life, the strain that giving birth six times in twenty years might have on a body.

Ena: you were a kind woman, a middle-aged widow, already set in your ways. You knew people all over the city and stayed in touch with the gossip and scandal of town and suburb. In this way, I seem to take after you. But it was embarrassing for us when we went to town with you in the school holidays; you'd stop people even if they didn't know you. Hello, don't I know you? The reading glasses quickly placed on your nose, you would peer into the face of the bewildered bystander. As if you weren't content with the company of your two grand daughters or wanted to show to us how popular you still were.

You were only sixty-nine when you died, but you were already worn out. In the doctor's rooms in the year before you died I sat in to offer some support. The general practitioner had never seen you before, and she was shocked at how much was wrong with you: problems with heart, lungs, kidneys, bowel, bladder, legs, eyes; diabetes, gout.

You carried a secret with you to your early grave. This baby, your first, born out of wedlock in 1929 in Fremantle. She found us not long after you died. As a family, in retrospect, we offered you so many cues to tell your secret, but you never did. That can't have been good for your health. It's not something easily forgotten, even after the birth of subsequent children.

None of us knows who the father of this baby was, whether he was a boyfriend, or a man who forced himself upon Ena; a married man or a family friend. Her address on this birth certificate is noted as Kojonup, also her place of birth, so it isn't too far-fetched to suggest the necessity for her to flee country-town shame to have her baby in Perth. This was one year before the death of her father, the beginning of her mother's forty-year widowhood. On the birth certificate of this baby, Ena is listed as *Eva Jessie*. Was this a diversion, a deliberate mistake to cover over tracks, or just some more blundering in the system of official record keeping?

White City

I am the grand daughter looking back and trying to make a picture with Ena in it at the start of her adult life. She lived her life in Perth and so have I. The central date in her narrative, 1929, is resonant in the historical milestones of this century and the place names are resonant for me. Hillcrest. Palmerston Street. The centre of the city. Town. By the time I knew her she was the age I am now. Our paths diverged from the first steps but we have both known this place intimately across our lives. It becomes my entry into Ena's drama of birth and relinquishment.

For a couple of years before 1929, arrangements were being made for the centenary celebrations of the settlement and foundation of the Swan River Colony. It was to be a grand affair. After all, it had been a difficult hundred years and some rewards, at least for perseverance, were due. There were extensive ruminations on how the milestone could be marked out: many grand schemes were proposed. This was a community that promised the earth but hardly ever followed through. Still, each school child was given one shilling. The Shenton Mill site was taken over as a public recreation area. There were centennial balls. A park was created. A centenary stamp was issued.

Before that, though, a bit of cleaning up was needed, particularly down on the Esplanade. In 1927 a temporary amusement park had sprung up on that stretch of grassy reserve. It was so popular that nobody rushed to dismantle it. The park had a little collection of names: White City, or the Ugly Men's Coon Town, or Carnival Square. A ramshackle set of buildings and sideshows; the lush grass soon became a filthy muddy patch. It was within cooee of the Supreme Court and Government House and, for that matter, the City of Perth and the Premier's office.

The Ugly Men's Association was a voluntary worker's group with a constitution and a president, Mr A Clydesdale, who was a member of the Legislative Assembly. The association had established White City to raise funds and it was successful; at first, the revenue was used for political purposes, the money going to Trades Hall, although that needed to be adjusted, or at least disguised by means of indirect money trails, once the authorities objected.

To those preparing for the centenary year, White City was an eyesore, would create a bad impression for special visitors. Hopefully the King would visit. There was pressure to close down the operation.

White City doesn't feature in much of the historical writing about Perth in the twentieth century. I stumbled upon White City by accident: a case of the mistaken identity of the leech gatherer at the Royal Perth Hospital — an Aborigine named Krakouer who needed free movement between the hospital and river, I had been told. I found out that in fact the man was not named Krakouer when I read through a box of documents, correspondence filed under "White City" in the State Archives.

The correspondence preserves contorted political arguments between State government and city council and licensing and church authorities. The Women's Service Guild, an early feminist organisation, objected on moral grounds and lobbied loudly to have White City closed down. The correspondence also refers to problems with the installation of septic tanks and lavatories, problems with the Swan River rising and the land along the Esplanade being too waterlogged to dispose of tank effluent. This was a battle between the Premier's Department, City Council and health inspectors, and returned them to the scandals of cesspits and double-pan systems and the typhoid deaths that had been such a problem at the start of the century. The tedium and boredom one senses in the tone of these files is likely to be in sharp contrast to how the battles were fought.

White City was an attractive site for many of the people of Perth. What they did there was the usual sideshow business: Boxing, Buck-jumping, Whippet racing and Games of Chance — Housey-housey and Sweat-wheels. Prostitution. Wild Beast Displays. All sorts of wickedness, I expect. Even some of the respectable members of the community were known to sneak in for its entertainments.

But when the Aboriginal people of Perth and the country started to frequent White City too much, it was time to step in and regulate, to monitor the movement of people. Already Aborigines were coming to the city to find work and seek assistance; a depressed economy had begun to hit country towns hard. A reserve had been set up in Guildford to keep some of these people out of the city, and other camps were set up in Swanbourne, Midland, Caversham, Lockridge and the Fremantle Cemetery. The increased presence of Aborigines in Perth caused much criticism, which was acted upon when the Governor made a Proclamation in March 1927 declaring under his powers that *the City of Perth be an area in which it shall be unlawful for Aborigines or half-castes to be or to remain.*[8]

The Chief Protector of Aborigines, Mr A O Neville, when asked by his counterpart in South Australia why this Proclamation was made, wrote that the problems started with amusement and ended in alcoholism and prostitution and the creation of disturbances.

If you care to check the official correspondence of the time, the to-and-fro between the office of the Chief Protector of Aborigines and the rest of the world, there are one or two anomalies that seem to spring from ideological differences. Mr Neville sent a memo to the police in 1927 urging that natives and half-castes be prevented from attending White City as well as barred from employment in or about the premises. The position of the police on this potential clampdown is surprising: they claimed that the Aborigines who visited White City were well dressed, of exemplary conduct, and did not fraternise with whites. They did not engage in bad behaviour, it was claimed, and they were not exploited by "low whites". Rather, Sgt Culmsec writes in his report to the Aborigine's Department, "I can see no reason why the pleasure and amusement they obtain by visiting this place should be curtailed or restricted."[9]

To counter any debasement, Pass Cards were issued to Aboriginal people with employment who wanted to be admitted into the city centre. Each was signed personally by the Chief Protector. Unemployed Aborigines didn't have passes and could therefore be picked up on the street and placed in custody. So could pass holders not carrying their identification.

blood relatives

In the south-west of Western Australia at the time there were two families of Aborigines with white fathers named Krakouer. It is hard to tell from this distance how much contact was maintained between the men and their children, and whether all of the children the women had were by the same man. It seems somehow unimportant. Depending upon what was at stake at any given time, these children were named Krakouer or given their mother's name. Often, they moved between different surnames. Some of them, called half-caste, were either half-siblings or cousins of Ena Krakouer from Kojonup. I imagine two of them, around the same age as Ena, coming to Perth in search of what was missing in Kojonup and its environs.

They join a camp in Midland and the next day they travel into town. It is a different introduction to the city than the white Krakouer sisters from Kojonup had: each in her turn, starting with Fanny and May and continuing with Nancy and Ena. These "other" Krakouers look around in awe at this busy centre and the big wide river and come home to the camp each night. They do this for weeks and then they are offered work in a market garden just out of Midland. In this market garden, the man grows tomatoes, cucumbers, watermelons and cauliflowers. One day when they are not required to work, they plan to walk into Perth and White City.

The young Krakouers from the country, visiting White City for the first time, are in gainful employment: Mr Bertonazzi can vouch for that if required, so it is quite legal for them to attend. It is a little like the Bridgetown Agricultural Show they went to last year, only bigger and with more activities. The Wild Beast Display and the Buck-jumping Competition are the highlights for both of them and their friends. They return home, exhausted after that long walk. Now that they are working almost every day, it is weeks before they manage to go back to White City.

Perhaps Ena Krakouer also attended White City. This may be where she met her boyfriend; it might have been the start of her love affair that ended with a pregnancy. Or she might have gone down there with her sisters now living in Perth or the friends she had made working in the tobacconist in Barrack Street, her first paid employment. That shop, T Sharp, was just across the street from the Bon Marché Arcade where Paul Le Comte was working in his fledgling business — repairing watches and clocks and occasionally adjusting out-of-style rings and necklaces to new designs. This was the bread-and-butter work of a watchmaker and jeweller — the chance to do original design a rarity in such straitened times. There is no romance here because Paul is still a married man and Ena is looking in a different direction, straight across busy Barrack Street. She knows nothing of the other Krakouers now living in Perth, who may be her cousins or even her half-siblings. Such stories are not spoken of in Kojonup and in Perth there is no need to even think about any bitter trace of potential relations if talk had ever got that far. Perth was a big centre with much more room than a country town could ever offer.

Ena and Paul

A man and a woman met and, despite the failures they had endured in the past, decided to marry and raise a family. They liked to enjoy themselves, to indulge their passions, to flirt and have the occasional tipple, to live a social life. The years had been tough and they had learnt how to make the most of everything. After one year of marriage they built a house in Como, had their first baby, and owned a car. Paul Raoul Le Comte, watchmaker and jeweller, operating from the first floor of the Bon Marché Arcade in Barrack Street, was born in Malta of a French father and Welsh mother; he stowed away to Fremantle when he was sixteen. His father was a professor of the French language at the University of Malta: that's what it says on his son's birth certificate. I ask my mother when I am growing up if Pop spoke with a French accent or an Australian one. It doesn't matter whom I ask, nobody can recover his accent from memory.

How did his voice sound?
Like Pop.

In the new British Library a machine on the wall contains Virginia Woolf reading a passage from her prose. I am intimate with her voice on the page, but this was shocking: she sounded terrible to me, her drone antithetical to the voice she usually constructs with language. For many English people it may be as expected, a normal upper-class English. The voice I have heard all of my life through accounts of Pop — Paul Le Comte — is an entirely assimilated Australian one. But I am sure that wasn't how he sounded to everybody.

When he was still a young man, he married and soon enough a baby boy was born. They lived in a shopfront in Beaufort Street but the marriage didn't last long. Some time after, he met Ena. When her half-brother, Paul's first left-behind child, was about to reach his seventieth birthday, my mother began to search for him, to phone him and wish him a happy birthday. She hadn't seen him since she was a little girl, and she considered seventy a significant milestone. But instead of phoning, she went to his house and knocked on his door and introduced herself as his sister. Now, with Ena's firstborn, she has three brothers and three sisters; two more than the family Ena and Paul set up in Como.

children

When we girls stayed with Nana I spent my days looking through all the treasures of the sleep-out, filled with Pop's papers and the things that he had coveted and invested himself in. Tucked up in bed each night I would read the *Reader's Digest*, trying to understand the intricacies of the Kent State Massacres and what the *Digest* was really saying about the students. It was the time that the richest girl in Perth was marrying a taxi driver and the story and photographs were plastered all over our daily newspapers. I wondered what it would be like to be getting married, or to be so rich, or to have such an ugly and forceful father. I think the *Reader's Digests* I read were at least a couple of years out of date, or otherwise they had remained fixated on the evils of student rebellion.

Nana lived in that house in that quiet street for years and years after Pop died. She was alone there, without sex or the close companionship of others living nearby, until a boyfriend came along. A man who cried and cried, was inconsolable at her funeral and then lost contact with the family before the year was out. Her own mother had been a widow for forty years. There were shifts in that street, slowly at first, as the old people died or moved into nursing homes and young people moved in and remodelled the family homes to make more floor space. Ena's main travel for many years involved the return bus trip from Como to the city along the Canning Highway. She gave up on visiting other suburbs early on.

Much earlier, in 1929, Perth was still, in many ways, a small British colony. Parochial, unsophisticated. Magisterial observance paid to the centenary celebrations. After a painful birth and coming of age, the celebration of a modern city. *It is hoped that the King will attend our anniversary.*

~

It happened to her in 1929, when she was nineteen. Her family and community judge her: she has behaved badly; violated moral codes. She has had sex with a man and the result will be a baby. She is not yet married.

The pure silence around that baby. Folding into itself. Providing an example for women further down the line. *Julie.* Keep it quiet. She had the baby and then took her home. A little girl she named Merle. They lived in Palmerston Street in the inner city in a house owned by someone in the family. Details are sketchy. She kept quiet about her experience, moved on from it, moved back into an old life and then commenced a new one as a married lady. Some people knew at the time, but everyone shut up after she gave her little girl away to be adopted.

When Ena's children from her married life, official and legitimated, began to have their own, some could not conceive and instead adopted. This might have been a perfect time to be able to tell her five children, or even one of them, that there was another sibling, another child of hers, to account for.

What might have happened if she had lived for one more year and met the fifty-year-old daughter who found us, too late, and entered the family? This new sister, previously unknown, was one of us. Distinctive resemblance: the same features, postural echoes. It was remarkable to meet her; it was as if she had rehearsed this entry all her life. And when it came, she fitted perfectly. She had always known she had a mother somewhere. What she found were the traces of her mother in the large family from which she had been exiled by adoption. She had been looking for her mother all her life.

Ena and baby Merle in Palmerston Street in central Perth in the year that Wall Street crashed and a world depression officially commenced. Tins of food in the cupboard, baby blankets borrowed from friends. The shame of the single mother walking the street with her baby in a pram. A fallen woman, fallen into disrepute. Palmerston Street is the street I drive down every day to get to my own house. She lived in my neighbourhood.

My terror. Streetwalkers, who cannot get jobs in brothels because they are too messy, not clean of drugs or cautious enough, have moved into my community, into the streets that form my neighbourhood. And changed it. Palmerston Street. Bulwer Street. Lake Street. Brisbane Street. They were moved out of another area when property values began to rise. Last week one of the working girls went missing. It takes many days to admit that she is not an "ordinary" girl who had been at the local pub — that she is a junkie — that she is a prostitute — that she is twenty — that her boyfriend dropped her off to work at midnight and didn't report her missing for three days — that she is the mother of two small children. "Street worker" is the euphemism for women who do business in the front seats of cars parked in laneways around here, or parked right there on the street. Forty bucks for a blow job and seventy for the full effect. The city erupts into people articulating their positions: property values; serial killers; moral imperatives; basic safety matters; heroin trials.

Ena kept her baby for nine months before she gave her away, before she handed her over to other people, before she arranged for her to be adopted out.

Saying goodbye to a first-born child. They won't meet again. As a woman who has never been a mother, I cannot imagine how this would have happened, the walking away, the pressures that forced her to make a decision, to forego a life with a child. *This tiny baby*. She must have looked like the next three who came in the next decade because they all share features as middle-aged women, the time that they created a relationship, when they took up being sisters.

What did you do? Make an appointment with the government to say: I cannot care for my baby any more, take her from me please. Or with a kindly old doctor in the neighbourhood who has been practising medicine and good advice since Adam was in short pants. *Yes dear, you made a mistake. Next time you will know better and wait until you are married with a nice house and a husband before you give yourself over to passion.* You hand over the little baby, nine months old, not knowing where she will go, but knowing it is no longer your business and that you have no responsibility. On the first night, the first Friday night, the first Saturday night, the first Sunday afternoon, what did you do, Ena? How did you arrange your time?

Such transgressions are to be found in most families if you dig far enough. If I'd known about it when I knew Ena as a grandmother, would I have been more sympathetic, more caring? I am taking my cues about her anguish from the accounts of relinquishing mothers I have read, but I might have it all wrong. It might not have been the trauma I imagine.

What an odd collection of things were found in her bedroom, in her wardrobe, when she died. They all seemed to have been stored up for some later consideration. The most remarkable items were two significant paintings by colonial artists. Who was the connoisseur in that family? I don't recall, ever, original artwork in the house for all of the years I knew it, and neither did my mother, who was born there.

I imagine that she kept one thing: a little gown in cream cotton with a delicate lace bodice. A kindly old neighbour gave it to her as a gift. I imagine that her first baby had worn it during their time together. It was kept in a paper bag in the bottom of her wardrobe at Campbell Street for nearly forty years. She never needed to open the bag, but she left it there for all of those years. When she died it must have been thrown out intact with the rest of the clothing in the wardrobe. Nobody would have thought it odd if they had investigated the garment; she was, after all, a mother of five, grandmother of thirteen.

My gesture of return to Ena is the baby gown, the imprint imagining it has made on my life. It is lovingly shaped and, importantly, it shows the signs of having been worn by an infant. It isn't dirty, not at all, but it has touched the delicate skin of Merle. It floats; a memorial of substance; the remembrance of a bond and two lives. It is too late for any other reconciling so I will use the materiality of clothing and the care of an infant as witness to her first act of maternity.

sounds like this

The utility of language. The bare bones of a dream. It's not a dream of unity but a desire for conciliation. For a sense of a family; the comfort I imagine possible in that unit of people. A community of blood. This is a dream. It also has an erotic charge, this following people in their private lives, in their fantasies and how they managed their difficulties. How they learned the repertoire of love and sex; how they made babies and then families; what their private spaces were like: bedrooms and kitchens and living rooms. Rooms of living. An evening fire and the family huddled around it with a cup each from the pot of tea. Their daily habits and routines and deprivations.

I enter the room and the effect of it is like a sound installation: my body's shape and speed activate an array of responses. Sensors placed in surprising places in the room will be set off only if I pass them in a particular way. It is a ghostly space, this, filled up with family, with their gestures and all of the detritus of their days and nights. What I find is contingent upon me navigating within the room, this ghost den. It always depends on which way I approach it. I make an elaborate dance to set off all of the sounds at once and as they disperse I start it up again in a new figure of eight.

I'm searching, sure; that is what I'm doing by writing. Searching for family. It's not that I want to live with them in their former world or occupy any of the spaces they once inhabited. I don't want to substitute my place for theirs. All I want is to find a little definition of the figures I have found inscribed in the handwriting of colonials, to see why we forgot them so swiftly.

answers without questions: Nancy Krakouer

This is what it is claimed she said, as reported in the *New York Times* on 26 May, 1942:

> Nancy Rachel Krakouer, a post office employee and the only woman among the defendants, was said to have suggested that the victims be tortured before being shot.[10]

In the proclamation of an "Australia First Government", which included a welcome for the Japanese and relief at liberation from the Jewish domination of Australia, Nancy is listed as the appointed minister of all women's organisations.

Nancy was interned. In my childhood when I was told stories of Nancy as a wild woman, the coda involved the punishment for being wild. Nancy had been deported for her bad deeds. I never asked where, as an

Australian citizen, she could be deported *to*, because I liked the mystery too much. Later — it always comes later — I read of her dislike of Jews, and her desire to see Roman Catholic priests put on road work and the church hierarchy shot. The *New York Times*, covering the trial, records that the group had drawn up a list of persons to be assassinated.

She was acquitted on the charge of conspiring to assist the Japanese forces, but ordered interned under national security regulations.

political adventures

Nancy is the only really notorious member of the Krakouer family, the only one individual who thoroughly made it into the records. She was a bona fide outlaw and my grandmother's younger sister. For years her name and photograph were printed in the newspapers of her provincial home town, the *West Australian* and the *Western Mail*. Day after day. No wonder she had to leave once she was a free citizen, released from long detention.

Nancy Krakouer, my great aunt, was a daughter of David and Jessie Krakouer. She died in Perth in 1985. She was a failed political activist and after the war she never tried anything like that again. She didn't talk about her past, either.

She fell in love with a man and she followed his calling. Perhaps she was simply lovestruck, smitten, and didn't think through the consequences. She is unlikely to have known about the logic of the Nazi Party at the time: that her two Jewish grandparents would have made her a *mischling*, first degree and therefore non-exempt from the Final Solution. It was lucky that the diaspora meant her father was born in Fremantle and not Krakow or Berlin.

The party she belonged to sparked a major political scandal across Australia, but this scandal involved a more considered exploration of ideas than the branch in Perth was capable of. The Eastern Staters were the intelligent ones and they really understood the terms of their bigotry; the Westralians were excitable. Nancy was really on the sidelines, not in the least bit important to any strategic operations anywhere.

Why she followed the path she did is a tricky question. Australia in the 1940s was full of bold political gestures. It was the middle of a war, fast and full of invention. She had the perfect alibi, though: it was love. She was in love with him before she even gave politics a single thought.

Were these people as serious as they have been made to appear? The Fifth Columnists. It was certainly an unfashionable position to hold in 1942 — to celebrate the actions of the Japanese as true patriots. Her infamy hits home in the highly charged Australia at the end of the century, which is wearing its racist simplicities boldly, and getting away with asserting them again in public. Graeme Campbell, previously a Labor politician, formed a new political party in 1996 and named it the Australia First Reform Party. Did he understand, when he echoed their name, that they intensely hated the British and admired the Japanese? The Australia First Movement — Western Australian branch. With only four members: a merry little band of rabid fascists.

But how maligned were they? Did this political stunt consist of loose talk and the drawing up of a wish list of social action? Without the means to do any of it? We, too, our merry little band of concerned citizens, have sat around for hours together, night after night, plotting the overthrow of our government. Some of us even know, crudely, how it works and how we might sabotage it. We are incensed, horrified, desperate at the rapid slide back. This government has no redeeming qualities. Racist. Lacking in humanity. Corrupt. If we were to be infiltrated by intelligence forces, would we, too, be charged with something? Treason? Something under the Security Act? Is it as easy as that to be labelled subversive?

Nancy. We called her Fancy Nancy because she had so much hubris in her. She could outdo everyone in everything. She cut my branch of the family out of her will because I laughed behind my hand at her over dinner and coerced my sister to do the same. That was the last time I saw her. It was adolescent behaviour and I was well past being a teenager, but I couldn't stop myself. Every family has a demon member, a difficult person who enjoys stirring up trouble. Nancy, returned to Perth in her old age to prepare to die, made many claims about how much she had — money and possessions — and how she would reward family for their care. Those people who would look after her.

When I was fourteen, I travelled to Melbourne and stayed with Aunty Nancy just as my mother had when she was fourteen. Nancy was kind to both of us. I knew that she was notorious, but I didn't know what she had done. I think I imagined that a sexual scandal had forced her move to Melbourne long before I was born. Nancy had recently retired from her job in a liquor store. She had pretensions about her position in the world, her intelligence and her superiority. She was a snob without a cause. She was also lonely, and seemed to enjoy my company, but didn't admit to either of these things. She took me to visit her friends on a couple of evenings, and we sat and played cards in their solid houses and apartments, and they served me cakes and themselves sherry.

It is only now I know about Nancy's past that I am intrigued that all of these people we visited were

Europeans, migrants from after the war. They all had thick accents and some of them, now that I recall, were undoubtedly Jewish.

I don't know what her interests were, or what these friends had in common with her. Perhaps they had been her customers in the liquor store. She talked incessantly about the luxury cruise liner she had travelled on last year with her friend Mr X. He was a minor television personality, anathema to all teenagers. He was short on talent and effeminate, and I wished that Aunty Nancy would stop talking about him being so special and maybe even her boyfriend, because I didn't believe the last part and didn't care about the first.

What was it like to be forced to leave Perth, her home town, because of her notoriety? To begin living in Melbourne, a city with many Jews? Did she change her mind about them, recant, accept her own Jewish heritage? It is hard to know because she never spoke of these matters, even after she returned to live in Perth in 1979 (the year I turned twenty; the year before Ena's firstborn reappeared). From the time she returned, she only spoke of the colour of fabrics for curtains, the distance from the city to Dianella in the bus, and hints of just how much money she had in the bank. She talked a great deal but told no one about herself. She fell into line in the family with her silence.

great-aunts

We laughed, my sister and I, at one malapropism and then couldn't stop. Laughed ourselves hysterical, and out of our inheritance. The honesty of our youth: she was a silly old duck, too full of herself, nothing in her to elicit our sympathy. Who cares; we laughed once, and then the laughter took over, bubbling up in our bellies. A disgrace for the real adults. She wrote us out of her will. If I had a second chance at this, I probably would not have laughed as hard. Not for the money, but to show a little more respect. These were not years when respect was a priority for me. When I first published a story that contained her name, a man phoned me to suggest that perhaps she was less culpable as a fascist than I was suggesting. It was likely more a matter for her of love, or lust. She had worked for Bullock before she joined the Post Office, and she "kept company" with him from June 1940. From August 1940 she worked at the Mount Lawley Post Office. Before this, in April, she had left her husband of two years, Reginald Norman Moss, because he was having a love affair and he wouldn't keep her financially any longer. It was also claimed, in official papers, that he was a drinker.

She lived at these addresses in 1942: 64 Pearse Street, Cottesloe. Manly Flats Flat One, 69 Terrace Drive, City. She moved there on Saturday 7 March, 1942, and she and Bullock were arrested there in the early hours of the next morning.

It is only now that I remember that Nancy fits into that category I named, of women in the family without children. Julie, me, Nancy. She married three times but didn't become a mother. I'll never know if she was infertile or if she decided she was not the mothering type. As part of her homecoming, in her first year back in Perth, Nancy was contacted by a woman on the telephone who declared: "I think you are my mother." "No dear," I imagine her saying, "that is out of the question." This woman was Ena's daughter, and Nancy provided her with the final clues that directed her to her mother, the now — but only recently — departed older sister of Nancy.

Be careful of confidence men; of tricksters; of Men From The East. The sisters warned me — my grandmother's sisters — and so did the sisters who followed them, my mother and her sisters. Aunty Nancy was the odd woman out — she had become a Woman From The Eastern States, an entity only a degree more respectable than their men. The Eastern States was just as much a threat to me as it had been for the colonists.

~

During my short summer in Canberra, in love and trying desperately to look like I was continuing my work, I spent time in the National Library and found Nancy's name in the room with a dim light that holds newspaper indexes, filing cabinets and microfiche machines. Four times she is listed in that year, 1942; it was shocking to read of her strong beliefs. It was reported that she wanted people tortured before they were killed and her list of victims was long: Jews, Catholic priests and hierarchy, the English. She would be the minister for all women's organisations in their provisional government. I held these photocopies close to me to remind me of home. I couldn't help thinking of her having been the ideal host for me in Melbourne when I was a girl.

Australia First

If there is one thing that Australian people can agree on it is racism. That is how the Federation was formed: against the odds, against reaching an agreement on federation, the problem of coolie labour galvanised all of the States into an understanding. During the gold rushes of the 1850s many thousands of Chinese arrived in Australia. Each of the States attempted to restrict such immigration, but all they managed was to anger England, which was trying to make a treaty of friendship with China and had policies to protect the Chinese from discrimination by any particular nation. The States kept trying to avoid the charge of this being a witch-hunt by including *African aliens* on their hit list of whom they didn't want. In all of the discussion about who wasn't welcomed in Australia, those who used their voices never mentioned Jews, who were, surely, as easy a target of vilification as the Chinese. By the middle of the following century, Australia First were the most vociferous opponents of Jews and their collective ambition of taking over Australia.

The drama around the Australia First Movement in 1942 carries with it questions about personal and cultural identity and Australian political thought. It started in Sydney with men and women in a quasi-intellectual setting. It resolved itself in Perth with people of strong convictions who had no idea how foolish they would appear. In Sydney the principal player was P R Stephensen, known affectionately as Inky all of his life, a Man of Australian Letters. He was a Rhodes scholar, a publisher, writer, editor and biographer, and a ghost writer. He was the editor and publisher of Xavier Herbert's monumental novel *Capricornia*. He started as a far left radical with his friend Jack Lindsay; he became a communist, and then a far right radical. He was born in 1901, the year of Federation. His patron was businessman W J Miles, who was prepared to put his not inconsiderable fortune into financing anything that attacked ideologies to which he did not subscribe. Jesus Christ and the British Empire were the first targets, but there were plenty more to come. Inky wrote a book called *The Foundations of Culture in Australia* and Miles published it in 1936. Its strong anti-British sentiment appealed to Miles. Inky was a friend of Bea Miles, his patron's daughter, the

Sydney eccentric well known for reciting Shakespeare in the streets and fighting taxi drivers and bus conductors.

Inky promoted a fierce nationalism that eschewed Mother and the Motherland, and insisted upon Australia growing up and into its own shape. He was deeply suspicious of Jews and had a strong line in anti-Semitism. Whenever anyone attacked him, he always made the same response, a blanket statement of dismissal: *We do not know whether he is a Jew.*[11] He promoted an alliance with Japan in a period, prewar, when there was a great fear of Japanese encroachment into Australia, and during the war when there was every chance that it might happen. Miles agreed with him on all of these matters.

Both of these men were fixated with Jews. Australia in the 1930s and 1940s was reacting to the refugees from Europe in a touchy way:

> we are compelled to recognise that some of the new arrivals, quite unconsciously, provoked dislike. Some had habits of thrusting themselves forward when they wanted anything, more than Australian manners and customs allowed. Some seemed, to Australian eyes, greedy. Some were openly contemptuous of the people they had come to live amongst. Such individuals were very conspicuous. They made it hard for themselves —

> and at the same time they made it hard for others, the more adaptable and better mannered of their kind — to win acceptance.[12]

Stephensen suggested support for Japan because it was the only country in the world free from International Jewish Finance. He and Miles prepared a case of causes and things to hate, and then started a publication called *The Publicist*, producing sixteen issues in five and a half years from 1936 until the death of Miles. They published translated speeches of Adolf Hitler, argued with everyone, and wrote densely repetitive prose, usually under a pseudonym. Because Miles owned the journal, he was allowed to indulge his verbosity and nobody stopped him, not even the Man of Letters who edited it. The aim of the journal was: "not to found a new political party. Our aim is limited to arousing in Australians a positive feeling, a distinctive Australian patriotism of a thoroughly realistic kind."[13]

Is this about a nation growing up? The early days of Australia First were full of grand claims but little action. In 1941 it began to get steamy: it was the middle of the war and there were serious threats of a Japanese invasion of Australia. Public meetings in Sydney turned violent and, while the Firsters continued to hold their strong convictions, they agreed, under pressure, to stop these meetings. At the last of their gatherings, Miles Franklin stood on stage as the guest speaker about to discuss nationalism. But she didn't get to talk:

after they sang "Advance Australia Fair", the Sydney Town Hall erupted in violence across ideological divisions, and she had to be bundled out the back door.

The Western Australian version of this story is one involving botched jobs and big egos. All of the action takes place over a short month. A man named Laurence Bullock, an Englishman who was working as organiser for the butterfat section of the Primary Producers' Association in the south-west of the State, big-notes himself to a dairy farmer named Edward Quicke and tells him he is the local organiser of the Australia First Movement. He isn't, but that is immaterial; Quicke's wife later reveals that "Ted and I used to take *Mein Kampf* to bed and read it chapter by chapter like the Bible." But before they even get started they are infiltrated by a police agent. Frederick James Thomas becomes a German named Hardt and meets Bullock and Quicke and Bullock's girlfriend Nancy Krakouer. There is another player for Australia First, Charles Williams, an insurance agent, but we don't hear much from him. Bullock is certainly the mouthpiece and the ringleader.

Hardt stirs them up and gets them talking in concrete terms and cranking up their fantasising. He pins them down, then hands them over to the Special Political Bureau of the Perth CIB. They make some stupid claims, but it looks from this distance as though they were indulging in political fantasy: unsophisticated, unsavoury, but not involving action. They wanted to welcome the Japanese, to knock off some people in power they didn't like, and some people who had slighted them. There were a couple of printers, both named Jarvis, from King Street who had dobbed Bullock in and got him into trouble with the police. These Australia Firsters were talking off the top of their heads in private and, without Hardt, they probably would have gone nowhere. They did not have the range of interests of the Sydney Firsters: of history and philosophy and the relevance of Nordic myths. Hardt infiltrated them on 13 February, and by 8 March they were arrested. Bullock lied all the way, but perhaps it could more sympathetically be called wishful thinking. He claimed that he had the south-west of the State already organised for uprising. Bullock and Williams were both English and had both settled in Australia under emigrant schemes that hadn't served them well. They both had axes to grind.

All four of these people were interested in excitement, in a change to the status quo, in being part of the action of war; but they chose to be on the side of the enemy. They were locked up from March to May and there was no public announcement until then about what had happened in the police court; they were held under section 13 of the National Security Act, later under regulation 26, and they were finally charged with an offence under the Crimes Act. Bullock claimed it was all a joke, a series of amusements made while they were still affected by a late-night drinking party. But there were papers. A set of principles. A map of bombs to be ignited: the Midland workshops, the Ford motor works in Cottesloe. A liquidation list of who would be shot. Bullock showed Hardt where the Japanese and German aircraft could land, and it was precisely the spot that White City had operated from, on the grassy part of the Esplanade. Japanese flying boats could land in Matilda Bay. *But Laurie, it's too shallow there! That's Perth's safest place for children to swim.* The atrocity stories about the Japanese were all "hooey and propaganda", according to Bullock. He wrote Nancy a love letter and in it he stated: "Enough of politics because Australia and Australians must now be educated by bombs or bayonets."

~

Nancy had returned to Perth at the age of sixty-four. It must have punctured her: returning to nothing much but with all the baggage of a long-ago scandal, and those nearly forty years passed living in another place. She had turned her back and walked into a new life and now here she was back in Perth. In the final six years of her life Nancy became a regular contributor to an evening talkback program on commercial radio. *Nancy* was well known to Graham Maybury on his "Nightline" show of opinion, hard-luck stories and local wisdom. She had a view on everything, so it was feasible that she could phone in every night to chat to

Graham. Nancy was sorely missed as a *colourful character* when she passed away in 1985. I am compassionate now, *in memoriam,* when I consider Nancy's loneliness, her stigma, her high expectations of herself and everyone else. The years she was locked in internment camps, imprisoned, took a toll that she likely never admitted. The past was just that, long departed and never conjured for anyone.

~

I will now form an Australia First Party said Bullock, and Nancy and Mr and Mrs Quicke all fainted with excitement. This was their means of becoming important in Perth. Miss Krakouer became the secretary because she could type a nice letter and knew where to post it. Williams didn't say much, but he did suggest sterilising all Jews to wipe out that social problem. And their Proclamation went like this:

> Men and Women of Australia: Today a new government assumes control of your destinies. Your government brings with it an entirely new system based upon a negotiated peace with Japan.
>
> The Australian nation is ordered to lay down its arms. The Japanese army of occupation will maintain law and order until such time as the government feel that the new system has been safely established.[14]

The Proclamation, however, makes no mention of the obvious need to abolish the White Australia Policy along with removing all Jews from government positions.

But this was precisely when it became serious. Because Bullock acted in a grandiose manner and spoke with a too-loud voice, a link between the West Australian four and the Sydney and Melbourne group was made. Sixteen overnight raids and arrests took place — from Inky Stephensen down. Many of those people were interned for periods of between a few months and three years. By then W J Miles was dead, so he escaped this ignominy.

Bullock's adventure fantasy became one of Australia's biggest national security scandals. There was an ersatz Royal Commission, an *Inquiry*; there was compensation; and there were twenty people locked up in internment camps — with Jews and with other reffos, all of them *not* Australian. The Australia Firsters soon set up an "Australia House" in their camp, and presented sixty-five talks in twelve weeks on subjects ranging from Gallipoli to the Stock Exchange. Stephensen called them simpletons, these halfwits from Perth, without having met them.

I am jagged by other details, like the names of some of the other people involved in this farce — Captain Blood of Military Intelligence; H J H Henchman, a military prosecutor. Nancy Krakouer, who was arrested by the police in the early hours of the morning in her flat in the company of her boyfriend Bullock. Every one of her sentences carried a dagger, and Bullock loved it. He loved a strong woman. Though the Commissioner of the *Inquiry into matters relating to the detention of certain members of the "Australia First Movement" group*, Mr Justice Clyne, said of them: "It is difficult to imagine what moved these puny conspirators to such ambitious and dangerous designs."

I am sure that they all felt credible and powerful, at least until they were sent to their internment camps. The Minister for Defence, it was established, could lock up anyone without any charge being preferred and there was no legal redress.

It is usual at a political meeting, Bullock had claimed, to begin with a preamble. *Quisling is the true patriot of Norway* was his suggestion, followed by *and we are the true patriots of Australia*. Everybody called everybody else a quisling in this scandal: sometimes as a compliment, sometimes as an accusation, sometimes as an insult. Quisling was made into a hero in Australia. Decades later it was still in place, this insult. The Quisling Quasimodo of Australian right-wing politics. When they all went to the Supreme Court of Western Australia, these true patriots, people were so excited that they forgot to take a shorthand record of proceedings for the sixteen days of the trial. The only record remaining of the trial is in the form of a report in the *West Australian,* which had already circulated it to the world as the strangest political story of the war.

I am more interested in the Englishman Bullock's internalised hatred, and in Krakouer, who came from a Jewish family, even if her mother disqualified her from being of the *purest* order. I am interested in all of the English-bashing, that striving for liberation which made allies of a whole range of different people. At the inquiry, when a young man named Gordon Rice continued to call Englishmen Pommies, the commissioner queried the use of the slang. Rice answered: "I called them worse than that when Larwood and others were here, throwing the ball at us instead of bowling."

In the Federal Parliament in 1946, Bullock and his partners were described by the Deputy Leader of the Opposition as "the gabblings of three or four windbags who had not the means even to stop a tram or kill a rabbit." Thomas, masquerading as Hardt, the police agent, the *agent provocateur,* was described as a pimp.

No wonder Nancy went to live in Melbourne.

love

She looks straight into the camera's lens. She is proud of her good looks and so she looks back without any shame. This is not the occasion for a smile but equally she doesn't want her straight line of a mouth to make her less attractive. So she makes a shape around her teeth; it's an O but not a smile, just a shapeliness for the bottom half of her face. It doesn't really work because it gives the impression that she has left her dentures out or that the photographer startled her just as he was capturing the image. She wears a natty hat with a modest feather attached to its band; she wears it back on her head and pitched slightly to the left. When she sees the photograph taken by the *West Australian,* she is pleased she chose to wear that hat. She congratulates herself that at the age of twenty-eight she still has girlish looks, especially around her eyes.

I've never been able to fantasise Nancy's adventure. Not effectively, anyway. Thinking about Ingrid Bergman in *Notorious,* remembering other women spies from Hollywood is exciting, but Nancy's tale is banal, leached of all interest. Is it just that her politics were so offensive? Anyone can make a mistake, once. Did she really know what she was saying? The plotting lasted such a short time and then there were all of those months that turned into years, three years for some of them, in custody.

The sheer silk stockings, held by a garter where it is warm and perfumed musky. The cut of the cloth of her suit is sleek and sophisticated. She smokes a cigarette; the room is illuminated by a blue light, ice cubes clink in a heavy glass of rich amber: Chivas Regal. Not bad for a girl from Kojonup, Western Australia, who has just moved into a modern apartment in Terrace Road, Perth, along the Esplanade and the Swan River. Married once already and now safely single and playing the field. Not young, but not yet past her prime. Aged twenty-eight. A Post Office employee, a woman of limited means.

She had, as we used to say, tickets on herself. Self-satisfied and wonderfully confident, she had a scent that attracted men. She spent her lifetime as seductress, flirting successfully wherever she went. This wasn't her first affair. She was in love with Bullock. He knew about politics and about solutions to practical problems. He had met his match with Nancy.

memorial books

I want to adapt an ancient form for my own purposes. I want to constitute memories, some of them straight out of the air, and make a picture of my own. Honour the distances between us.

The memorial book, the yizker bikher, *"tombstones of paper", often concluded with a list of the names of the dead, a reminder about the dangers of forgetting. It contained collections of details, writing in skin and scraps, from a community and its living: the prosaic and the almighty, the marks of its existence. Inscriptions offering collective memory, comforts during expulsions, annihilations, simple vilifications. They held local histories, mixing up daily transactions into a system of record keeping. Bearing witness. Invoking the dead, paying them what they deserve in the form of remembrance and all of the obligations of those who follow. Naming and detailing the treasures from life: sculptured trees surrounding a town, the sound of the congregation praying, or mourning, or having fun.*

Since the European Holocaust, memorial books have come into their own, standing solidly for tangible detail in the face of devastation. When entire communities went, without ceremony or burial; when tradition was obliterated, this enactment on paper became a singular recuperation, charged with symbolic strength.

I compile names and try to make a list. I want to write my memorial book about just one family, my family. Is that allowed? And if it is, does it matter if I embellish what I know? There is so little evidence remaining in the world.

This is my song of yearning.

Theodore Krakouer. Brina Israel. David Krakouer. Jessie Krakouer. Ena Krakouer Le Comte. Nancy Krakouer. May Krakouer. Julie.

Books and learning are so central to the Jewish people. This idea enables me to write into a new confidence. My grandfather, not a Jew, was as passionate about information and its collection and about books. All his adult years he spends time and money, a considerable amount, in his collecting: it is a hobby that has taken over his life. He lives for it. How did your family feel about it, Pop? When passions are not shared, it must be lonely. And it must be difficult for family to understand the compulsions and pleasures and importance of a pastime that takes you away from them, and uses up money for clothes and movie tickets and perhaps even a visit to Luna Park.

My grandfather, Paul Le Comte, had this passion, all to himself. His big scrapbook was labelled "Something of Interest" and was filled with autographs of Hollywood stars who travelled to Perth; with letters from the Queen and the Historical Society; with the original miner's-rights certificate Paddy Hannan was granted; with pressed flowers and badges of honour. He left them all in his little house in Campbell Street when he died. They were for the pleasure of looking at, a constellation of ideas, this random selection by one man. Books were as precious to him as they are to me; most of the family can take them or leave them. This is our connection, a posthumous one.

The imprint of intimacies carried in those books, a palimpsest. When I look through the books I can see the hands of Paul, his children, his friends, some of his grandchildren.

remembering and forgetting: Aunty May

She isn't sure who she is anymore and here we are sitting and asking her questions and forcing her into small talk. And she keeps asking us

who are you?
how do you know me?
why are you here?
have I met you before?

Over and over and over.

But she isn't interested in answers.

Hers is a better class of nursing home. In the institutions for old age, residents and staff get used to all the smells and the floors are so shiny that each spill is easily cleaned up. For visitors it is hard every time: those pungent smells of food cooking and being served is countered by the sharpness of bleach and disinfectant.

May is immaculate. She grooms herself well every day and insists on help from the staff when she can't manage. At her ninetieth birthday party she looked like a sweet little doll in her best dress, brooch, scarf. She was colourful and crisp as she has been all her life.

The way she remembers. The stops and starts in the narrative of her life. She stops herself. It is a compelling rhythm, all that repetition. Like the music of minimalist composers. Stop. Start. Go for a burst. Stop. May makes a mesmeric beat just with her pauses.

Behind her bed, hanging on the wall, are framed photographs of sons and grandchildren. They are the only mementos she has carried with her into this final home. When she sits up in bed, as she does for long periods of each day, she looks upon another treasure taken from her former life. It is a dramatic portrait of Ingrid Bergman as Joan of Arc: victorious, proud, a perfect Hollywood image from the past.

The portrait dominates the small room with its low ceiling. May is asked who the lady in the photograph is. She is unsure — mother, sister, daughter. No, she didn't have a daughter. She wants to say it is May. The shifting nature of her memory obscures this treasure she has owned for so many years, since the 1940s. It hung in the lounge room of the family home, now sold and all contents disposed of. A big photograph of a woman burned at the stake. The film still is from a scene before the immolation, though. She sits astride her horse, in her armour. She is beautiful and purposeful.

May is one of two left from her generation; she is an old, old woman. She is the grand daughter of Brina and Theodore Krakouer. My great-aunt. Her final home is the Masonic Nursing Home in a suburb of Perth; she has come here after living her adult years in the south-west and in Perth. The nursing home is a place for the ordinary grotesque: old men push themselves around narrow corridors for exercise and entertainment. There is a general decay of bodies and minds. As memory fails, they live quite in the present. Most of the pleasure is located in the past.

There is a tandem team, a husband and wife both in wheelchairs, who move about and argue in the way they probably have all their life together. They wait for other people's visitors because they have none of their own anymore. They wait to hijack new people to talk to: the woman asks for a push, and then the man, who was doing a fine job pushing his wife and wheeling himself, is deeply offended. Brooding, he ignores his wife and the stranger; he has been emasculated in the corridor.

May is in a room of her own. There is a wilful streak still in her face. She has always been a cheeky woman, a stirrer, defiant. It is hard to know what she is being defiant about, it seems to be her general demeanour. She has dementia, Alzheimer's disease. Looks people straight in the face and repeats every question they ask her. Throws it right back and, because of her quizzical look, it is hard to know if it is the cheeky woman or the disease talking.

May is being interrogated about her childhood and her family. The family historian has visited, earnestly, with the tools for stimulating memory: with photographs and stock phrases, names and relationships. These days May is stuck on her questions of *who* and *why*, which she asks every couple of minutes. Between times, though, there is some lucidity. There is a photograph of her as a little girl, five years old, with her parents, some siblings and other adults. She is asked about her childhood: the great-niece tries to reach those memories of far away that may hold more significance than the place May is trapped in right now, this delusional space where she can't hold a thing, not even the last question answered. She identifies everybody in the photographs: Mother, Grandmother Patterson, Father, Grandfather, herself, her sister Fay and brothers Raphael and Abraham, a cousin. The questions asked about these people: what was your mother like? your father? were you happy?

She answers directly, the only direct thing she has to

say, that it is too late, that she has now forgotten it all, all such detail. It is too late. Sorry.

Do you dream about your mum and dad?
Yes, I do. I still do.
I want to write a story about our family.
Oh why? They were very ordinary. Nothing more than that. My mother was kind and good. My father was blind. Yes, he was good too, a kind and gentle man, even after he went blind.

It is too late. There is no such place as a family archive, a place where knowledges have been stored.

Her father, David, was Brina's baby, her ninth child. In other narratives of Perth there are tales of a blind violin player in a small country town who in the Depression once travelled to Perth to play his violin on street corners to collect a few morsels to keep on living. In other words, the man had begged. This story has cut across family mythology in a most peculiar manner. David was blind, but he didn't play the violin and he didn't need to beg. The truth is that he was dead right after the onset of the Depression, in 1930, at the age of sixty-one, that he left money in a will and wasn't destitute. He had married when he was twenty-nine, and in 1930 had adult children. He had been a farmer in Kojonup and before that owned a wagon and team and carted for the goldmines in Kalgoorlie. But when he was stricken with blindness he moved into the town of Kojonup.

I requested the death certificate from my usual source. David's father, Theodore Krakouer, is named as a storekeeper and, for once, both of his parents' names are spelt correctly. David is buried in the Church of England section of the Kojonup Cemetery and his profession is listed as *Pensioner*. All of his children, aged between thirty and sixteen, are named, as is a deceased male baby. I read the column Cause of Death. *Tabes Dorsalis. Uraemia. Heart Failure.* I understood the second two ailments, but the primary cause of death was confusing. From the sound of those words, all I could think of was sharks swimming in the ocean, circling around a target.

When I showed the certificate to a friend who is a doctor, I realised that it could all come falling in on the family. Tertiary syphilis. This was also what had killed his father, my grandmother's grandfather, fifty-seven years earlier. But it wasn't inherited from Theodore or his own children would have been affected. His syphilis was all his own. Our culture can talk a little more freely about sexual health these days — it is not the stigma it once was — but no family wants this sort of information. His wife Jessie died after forty years as a widow, but two of his daughters were still living.

These are the symptoms of syphilis, the way the body is ravaged by the disease. First, a primary shancre develops on the genitals or in the mouth. Then it clears. Within six to eight weeks there is a new set. Second come fever, headaches, spots, pustules which disappear slowly. Then tumours in skin gummata, changes in the body, including the bones. These changes affect the brain and result in paralysis of the face and lower limbs, a loss of coordination. A straddling walk. Blindness. And then death.

Theodore dies of syphilis in 1877. Then his son, David, in 1930. Both die of this disease: *Tabes Dorsalis*.

other taboos

By a meandering path through books and loose talk about colonial days I arrive at another taboo. This one seems to be the most powerful transgression of all within the family, one that I pejoratively and deliberately name as miscegenation; it is still such a silence that it eclipses every other one of the transgressions: the convictism, the madness, the illegitimacies, the Judaism in a Christian community, the disease. And I am thinking, what is the next move when every move is equivalent and each of them involves a reward and a risk? This is the type of subject to be warned off: I already have been by people in the family who I barely know, who name it as my muckraking or as simply untrue, or as an act of saucy rebellion. So I turn to the authorities for support:

> *Miscegenation*: As it pertains to Australian society, it began at Sydney Cove in 1788 with the first sexual relations between white men and Aboriginal women. Reports from the interior of New South Wales in the 1830s emphasised that virtually every stockman had an Aboriginal "wife" and that infanticide of part-Aboriginal babies was common. Various governors, commencing with Arthur Phillip, vainly attempted to prevent these relationships in the belief that they caused much of the violent conflict on the frontiers of settlement. During the first half of the nineteenth century this interbreeding, while considered socially demeaning, was seen by some observers as improving the original racial "stock".[15]

~

Paul Keating's Redfern speech in 1992, which referred to the sins of the past and of acceptance of these to move towards a reconciliation of Aboriginal people with non-Aboriginal people, was the first occasion some of these ideas had been spoken in public by an Australian leader.

It is puzzling how long some things take to sink in. The words that the Prime Minister used in public on that day were like a body blow to many viewers of the television news. Murder. Disease. Failure. "As a consequence, we failed to see that what we were doing degraded all of us."[16] This wasn't about party politics and it certainly wasn't about votes. "We fail to ask — how would I feel if this were done to me?" He spoke the shame directly, a national shame that had not yet publicly identified itself, and something began to shift.

That *we* in his address was provocative because *he* was the leader and this was an act of leadership. That word *smashed*. Keating said a great deal in that speech: he said it was *our* ignorance and *our* prejudice, he took some responsibility for identifying this *our.* "We took the children and we swapped them for alcohol and broken health and dispossession." He used the word *traditional* — took and smashed what was traditional. And he framed it in a simple discourse: "we failed to make the most basic human response and enter into their hearts and minds, most of us." And named the exceptions, those people who made that leap of faith, across race and understanding, as *noble.*

And I read another quote that uses the word *smashed* to describe action:

> We thought it was only the blackfellows who smashed things because they drink too much and become a little bit wild. Culture in official Australia, begins not with Indigenous peoples, who have been suppressed and exterminated, but stems from British culture, brought hither by Englishmen, Irishmen, and Scotsmen throughout the Nineteenth Century.[17]

I am in a fug from reading the discussions since the start of the nation, the counter-histories, the eyewitness accounts. I absorb catchphrases and could parrot back to you any number of theories about race and the establishment of Australia; it keeps me awake at night.

> The culture of a country is the essence of nationality, the permanent element in a nation. A nation is nothing but an extension of the individuals comprising it, generation after generation of them. When I am proud of my nationality, I am proud of myself. My personal shortcomings, of which I am only too painfully aware, are eliminated to some extent by my nationality, in which I must justly take pride — such is the reason for nations and nationalities, and also for tribes, mobs and herds.[18]

There has been in such a short time some loosening up of the anxieties about mixed blood. Some white people have even begun to look for Aboriginal links in their family chain, and welcome such surprises. Shame can be dispersed when we share stories; when they are spoken. Where once the stories of the British majority were the dominant stories of our culture, now it is the stories held along the edges that begin to be heard. Often for the first time. When stories about families being forcibly split up are spoken beyond trusted sources, out into a wider field of listeners, compassion is often the first emotion activated.

Maybe the public recognition of a convict past that only began to be uncovered and talked about in the 1970s was a practice run at this. When convicts began to be seen as contributors to the development of the nation, the shame associated with a convict passage to Australia by a forebear was lessened, even turned into pride. But this is more profound: this opening up that tells of State racism and racist laws being enforced at the same time as the white men who wrote them into the statutes have intimate relations with the women of that race. So it is also about hypocrisy. The white men stopped having sexual relations with their white wives when they caught venereal diseases, and the black women and men were locked up in hospitals, called lock hospitals, away from everyone else. These details now, recently, are part of our popular understanding of the past.

For so many years when Aboriginal people were identified with the mark of British names, for generations, it was always explained as the practice of the blacks taking the name of their bosses or masters. That white masters named their property was obvious: it is too easy to lose something you own if you don't mark it as yours. The mark of the oppressor. And people believed it. So when I started thinking of my family line, the Krakouer family, in the 1980s, and the famous football players Jimmy and Philip Krakouer became heroes, I was assured that it was because their grandfather or his grandfather had worked for David or Rudolph or Raphael in the South-West some time around the crossing of the centuries.

~

Maude phoned me one month after her mother had passed away. Her mother had gone into hospital and read my entry in the Can You Help? column of the *West Australian* newspaper asking for any information about the Krakouers. She wanted to contact me, and asked her daughter Maude to do so; she had wanted to share her Krakouer family stories with me. But then Maude's mother became seriously ill and passed away quickly. In the flurry of sadness and the need to make practical plans, Maude didn't phone me for a month. We didn't meet for another three years, but it was worth the wait.

I visited Maude at her home in Mandurah and walked in on another family history centre. Most of it was in her head: an immaculate record of genealogy, of the lines of family. There are few people I have met who can store in the mind people and their relations to others as Maude does. So here I came to another site of yearning. An idea of family, and the bonds each person has with siblings and parents and nephews and nieces and cousins. At this place there was room in the heart of the family even for the failures; there were no outcasts. Maude embraced me as a cousin even though she had only just met me. She was prepared to accept me through our link of blood, our parallel families.

Years ago I had come across a book of the genealogies of South-West Aborigines, the Nyoongars. Across a century or so of collection I found reference to my great-grandfather David named as the de facto partner of Sophie Smith, the father of her children. Back then, I had quietly closed the book and kept it to myself. It felt like a time bomb; I didn't want to detonate it. Besides, it could too easily be dismissed by the family. They named the wrong man. Well, maybe they did. Maude's mother Irene, directly descended from David or one of his brothers, lived out in bush camps for much of their time together so that they could stay together as a family. There was always a risk of being split up, of the kids being sent to Carolup or another mission.

Old Jesse E Hammond surfaces again in my reading of Western Australian history. Years before he drew his map of Perth he had:

> lived and worked in the south of Western Australia during the second half of last century. He was semi-literate and his observations of Aboriginal life during this period were recorded by Sir Paul Hasluck who was then a reporter with the *West Australian*. These reminiscences were published under Hammond's name in 1933 in *Winjan's People*.[19]

~

This is an Australian story of family; it is the sort of story that hasn't been told until recently. We have been living with myths to keep the truth at a distance. Myths of pioneers and benevolence and the barriers that were erected between black and white, between races. There is no unity yet. Each pause, if added up, would last the length of a symphony. And it is so hard to know how to approach it, this material that speaks shame. The business of biology, of family tracks and traces. One part of the family is Jewish; it starts off that way at least. Another part is Aboriginal. An Australian experience; a colonial experience. The quintessential Australian family. How do we get back together? Does one experience diminish the other, or compromise it? Nyoongar people marked by a name that stands in for a place, Krakow, an ancient city in a country that so recently obliterated its Jews. How does that mark of a name and a bloodline stand up in a Native title claim — does it diminish anything, and if it does, can you explain why?

Krakouer sightings

Other people have already taken the role of archivist of the Krakouer family in Australia. For years now, since the start of my research, people have been helpful and provided me with clues to the family path. Snippets sometimes misheard, sometimes wrong-headed — I listen to them all and record them. Some of these tales have directed me to useful material, but not always. The tumult builds, the notebooks grow, filled with contradictory stories told by now-anonymous informants.

> *Oh, you must be related to old Mr Crawcour. He was such a civic-minded old man. Came from Melbourne, had been here in Perth for ever. A lawyer, or an accountant, as I recall. He had one son, at least. You must make contact.*

Picture this. A boy starts his working life in the seedy part of Perth, in Roe Street, in 1945, in a second-hand building materials warehouse. He is seventeen, obsessed with girls but knowing nothing about sex and is unacquainted with any girls. He dreams about them all the time. Roe Street is hot, blank, uninteresting, despite the promises of brothels with names like *Silver City*. Each time the steam trains pass there is cheering and shouts and yells from the troops returning from demobilising camps. At first the boy rushes out, imagining something exciting has happened. But nothing; it is a private code that excludes him. One day, however, the noise from the troops reaches a crescendo and he rushes out to see what has happened. He tells it in this way:

> In the centre of the road outside the Josie Bungalow stood this lady; she was large, tall, big-boned (whatever that means) but she was big and was what my dear old mum would have called busty. I probably wouldn't have called her that because I would have been covered in confusion at the need to describe such attributes. But she was! She stood facing the train, legs like tree trunks set apart and hands placed hard on her hips with spine straight and head back. She was dressed in a pair of scarlet tights, that's all, and she swung rhythmically from the hips, her bare breasts being flung slowly back and forth as the train steamed by.
>
> The effect on the rude soldiery was spectacular; upon a callow youth with no experience of the female form it beggars description. I ran back

inside; harm, I thought, could come to a young lad if he wasn't careful.

Some time later a customer came to arrange purchase of some building material. She seemed familiar and the atmosphere within the ranks of my elders in the office became sort of electric and edgy and oddly respectful. I watched with averted eyes in the certain knowledge that she came from that house and that she was that woman. On making out the dockets I noticed her name; for no reason that I can see it stayed with me these fifty years or more. Krakouer it was, Mrs Krakouer.[20]

~

A woman in the 1970s contacted my second cousin wanting to sell him her book about the Krakouers, a family history. She was almost finished; had been researching it for close to ten years and now wanted some return for her labour. Nobody had asked her to write this family history, but she was indignant when my cousin refused to pay the ten thousand dollars. As her price fell, his suspicion grew. What are her motives, he asked himself. She returned to finish her work in the Battye Library, the State's historical library, but she was unhinged. Miss X caused problems for staff and other researchers, and had to be removed from the building more than once. She changed her name by deed poll to a much fancier one, and later she was committed to a psychiatric hospital. I think she is still there, but it is hard to confirm such information. Her parting gesture involved donating her papers to the Archives. But she arranged a fifty-year embargo, expiring in 2043, on the papers about the Krakouer family, her hard work. Conflicting stories circulate in this small community about those papers and what they contain, whether there is any real evidence anyway.

She was not a member of our family. Her interest is a mystery. What she found will remain a mystery for another five decades. Fellow researchers make wildly variant claims about her work: that the Krakouer manuscript, ultimately, was not part of her deposit; that she fiddled with her papers and changed them significantly while she was on day release from the hospital; that she identifies as a victim of repressed memory and when she remembered what happened to her as a little girl she chose a notorious family to hide behind. She buried herself in paper, in facts and wild hypotheses.

~

Early on in my search for detail, I place an advertisement in the daily newspaper asking people to contact me with information and anecdotes about the Krakouers. There are many telephone calls in response, with conversations about particular individuals: about Theodore, David and Nancy. I receive a letter from a man named Krakouer who claims to have a store of knowledge, a lifetime of research that he is willing to share with me. So I travel to visit him in his small town out of Perth. I expect to spend the half-day with him; he expects to live the rest of his life with me. He is a lonely old man who had anticipated my visit more than I could ever imagine.

I arrive at 9 am on a Saturday and enter the rudimentary flat he lives in alone. He already has the pot of stew cooking and ready on the stove. I decline his offer of a plate for breakfast. We talk for an hour or so and then we walk to the pub. By now he is shaking. It is the latest start he's ever had to a day's drinking. He is mad: he is only interested in the splendours of the family, the buried treasure and the aristocratic links he claims he can trace. Mr Krakouer claims the world: that we have the first white baby born in a certain town; the first Jewish baby born in Western Australia; the biggest and always the best of everything. But never with any evidence. His research is fantasy; the papers he holds insubstantial, inauthentic, mostly scraps of yellowed envelopes recycled with hieroglyphs and single words and numbers. His brain is addled by booze and regret and he tells me he is suffering from a *medical condition.*

I feared from the start that he might kidnap me. One image stays with me: a photograph of him with a woman at a formal party in the 1960s. She looked so vile and conniving that I wasn't surprised when he told me, salaciously, the spit forming in his mouth's folds, she was a bad woman, very naughty. Yes, very naughty.

~

There was another man named Theodore Krakouer who lived in Sydney in the 1970s and who had spent all of his money on the costs involved in preserving his parents' bodies in a funeral parlour. His parents were named Theodore and Brina, and they were cousins who had met and married in Victoria in the early twentieth century. Theodore Krakouer and Brina O'Reilly. They married in 1928, on 3 May. Theodore was the son of Abraham Krakouer, Theodore and Brina's firstborn, the mythologised first Jewish baby born in Western Australia. Brina O'Reilly was Rachael Krakouer's second-born daughter. Rachael was Abraham's sister who had left the Swan River Colony early and settled in Melbourne, marrying a butcher in Carlton called O'Reilly.

Eventually, the money dried up and the two long-deceased bodies had to go somewhere: into the ground or burned? The customer had been a firm believer in cryogenics, but this loving son could feed his habit, or faith, no longer. Those bodies had been stored in the funeral parlour for twenty years. So the story goes.

~

Another informant tells me of a photograph she has only heard about but was prepared to contribute to family myth. Its subjects were a dainty woman in Victorian dress, prim and white, and a big black man in tribal dress. Dressed to kill, presumably. A certain Miss Krakouer, the daughter of Theodore and Brina, in the late half of the nineteenth century, with her husband. I would love to see this photograph, but I fear it might be the construction of a fantasy of equality. If the white men could have black women, why couldn't women do the same? It is the tribal dress that leaves me suspicious, unconvinced. The myth of the savage man tamed by a Rachael or a Fanny or a Phoebe.

The pronunciations: Krack-hour. Crack-over. Krak-ooer. Cracker.

~

Sending out letters across the world to America, Sydney, London, Brisbane, Poland. Nothing ever comes back. Just the instruction on envelopes to *return to sender*.

Sometimes amazing stories come my way, but they only ever arrive as coincidences, and none of them can be substantiated.

> In the winter of 1976 violence spread to the heart of Perth. On Saturday night, 10 July, John

> Krakouer, a part-Aboriginal, ran for his life through the middle of town pursued by a dozen others. They caught him at the corner of Hay and William Streets and beat him to death with sticks and broken bottles.[21]

In the business of historical research, I am a failure. There are other people with a fascination with the facts of this family, with collecting the evidence of a lineage. Not all of us are related, but we have all met, with not as much to exchange as you might imagine. I wonder if their passion for the family has sent some of them around the twist. Can a researcher become contaminated by her material?

Sighting

The climate affords us ample visits to the beach for most of the year. We swim in a buoyant and clean ocean and the only collective fear involves sharks and shark attacks. These happen rarely. In this salty mass the blue of sky and water merge, or, at least, reveal themselves in such subtle gradations that they seem to merge. The effect is effervescent: in delicious contrast to the parched spinifex along hot bitumen of the route that has brought us here, like every other surface for our local transport.

To live in Perth you must tolerate flatness and harsh surfaces. As long as you have your eye always on the lookout for water this is possible. There is a stretch of Hay Street, a long road that runs through the city, where you can see the ocean ahead of you and, in the rear vision mirror, the clump of hills that look down on the city. Other than this platform and some variability around sections of the river, Perth has a relentless flatness that guarantees you feel like you are travelling forever along roads and across wide intersections.

Brina's body

It came in a dream but really it was from waking life. A chain effect, a reaction; a movement that could be called a symphony. A symphony of gestural inflections. A most subtle thing. A family, gathered together around grief, but at the same time carrying a range of other expressions. Joy and forgiveness; the pleasures of possession and love; the observation of the utterly new movements of a first baby each and every day — a child who is grandchild and nephew, too. But there is an imperative, for the sake of respect, to set aside all of these things and arrive at the loss in a concentrated manner, properly and fully. This necessary grieving. For some, the upswelling takes time and they watch their fellows weeping from a curious distance before joining this wet memorial.

All of her children were fully grown when she died. Her husband would have been there at Karrakatta Cemetery, but it is hard to make a list of any others who attended. It was in 1902, after forty-nine years in the colony. Were there friends made during the long sentence of those years? Is it a luxury to have friends?

Her grave sits there in the Jewish Orthodox section of Karrakatta. It took me a while to find it, a couple of visits to work out the numbering and find the modest plot filled in with blue granite pieces. Unmarked, and the cemetery board cannot tell me whether or not there has been a gravestone at any time to mark her death. All around her are monuments of grand dimensions: crypts, almost, honouring the life of the patriarch, the matriarch, the children lost early in the wars, the ordinary members of each family, the mark these families made on their community. Seeligsons and Brecklers and Solomons and Freemans.

This is my epitaph for Brina, retrospective, truncated, unengraved:

> Here lies Brina Israel Krakouer Mardon
> Sister of Esther and Abraham and Hannah
> Daughter of Samson Israel
> Beloved Wife of James Mardon
> Mother of Abraham, Phoebe, Rachel, Fanny, Sampson, Rudolph, Philip, Raphael, David Krakouer.
> She Lived a Hard Life and She Kept Her Spirit.
> She Loved Well.

> Born London 1833, Died Perth 1902, Aged Sixty-Nine.

I return to her and share pleasures I have known. I imagine her as a woman who loved.

1853

Brina Israel arrived in Australia by choice. She was nineteen years old. Years later, at the age of forty-one, she wrote a letter to the man holding the highest post in the colony. She implored, and she declared *I will not go to the Poor House again.* She had been there with her children, more than once; that was enough. When she and her sister Esther, sixteen, left London, there was no one to wave them away with good wishes and happiness and tears and shouts. They left alone; it was a banishment of sorts. Esther was expecting a baby and they left to get on with the pregnancy and her baby and their new lives as far from London as they could imagine. At the dock, scenes of choreographed grief and good wishes by other people were being enacted. They participated and waved into the void of loved ones; they went along with the spirit of the event, this flamboyant farewelling.

They named the baby Emma Alice. I don't know where she was born. She is in the official Australian records for every other event of her life but her birth.

1864

In the poorhouse. An infernal place at the top of the hill overlooking the settlement of Perth and its winding river. Filled up all the time by people who cannot ever seem to manage. Money is the problem, always, not enough to go around. The poorhouse is crawling with human misery. Children sullen; women, the mothers, hysterical. Feeling much put upon to be in this terrible colony with none of the help or respect that should be expected from life. This is the hardest thing, ever. And hot, an inferno. No wonder that infants perish and poor old drunks curl up their toes and die. Swan River Colony wasn't imagined as anything much beyond its potential development of capital: "The object of the colony was to let money make money. The senior officials and leading settlers of Swan River were men of means, not mendicant refugees from the old world."[22]

This was the first time in the poorhouse for them. Brina (age thirty-one), Abraham (eleven), Phoebe (nine), Rachel (eight), Fanny (six), Sampson (four), Rudolph (one). Seven people from one family whose numbers would swell by another three. The missing member is the one who gave them their name, Krakouer. Theodore (age forty-six). Father and de facto husband and currently on a charge before the Supreme Court. What did he do this time?

Brina. You are my construction now at the end of the

century you died in. All I have as evidence of your long residence in the place I was born into is your name on some certificates: the births of your children, and the deaths, and a couple of historical notes on researchers' cards in the State Archives. And the series of your letters to officials on microfiche.

The silences of the past can be too easily filled with concerns about the present, and come to carry these concerns. I am trying to listen, closely, to murmurs; to sidestep the tumult, the shouting, all of the monumental gestures. I want to pare this drama of genealogy right back to bare bones, to keep perspective, avoid hysteria.

I want to know what Brina looked like but there is nobody to tell me. It is a sentimental tool of connection, a point of identification; I want to know if she looked like the rest of us. There are no photographs. What I found in the State library, more resonant anyway, are copies of her letters. These writings, in her loopy hand, tell me many of the things I want to know. My embellishments originate from her modest letters, heartfelt, pleading, compelling.

Having seen one photograph of her youngest child, my great-grandfather David, when he was an adult, I construct her physical shape, her distinguishing features. By the age of thirty-six, near enough to my current age, she had nine living children, her first born when she was twenty. By the age of forty-four she was widowed. Brina was resilient; I think she must have won the fight she had with the authorities. Won it at least by maintaining her stance.

So, what did she look like? I'll give you the picture forming out of my neediness. It is, plausibly, from her life in Perth, not before. She is little, a tiny woman even before she began to shrink. Dark hair, penetrating eyes, a long nose, a quick wit, a sharp temper. I am reading her letters closely and still coming up with a set of clichés. A discomfort with the climate: it gave her prickly heat in her armpits and inner thighs, made her prodigious child-bearing painful in her skin and throughout her body. Gave her a roughened face, ruddy, hard-complexioned. She went grey early, craved space for herself, wore her hair long. Dreamed of her father and mother, wondered how it was that she and Esther had taken this adventure as young women.

I walk along a street of the town and there is a most remarkable explosion of sounds. At each step is a new bird song, sometimes a screech of humour or heartache. I am sorry that I do not know the names of these species. There is the shaking of trees, the crackle underfoot of foliage, of leaves and grasses and also crickets. I know no names yet to describe any of these things aside from bird, tree, cricket. It is a new world. This world is alive.

Dainty, dark and delicate. The two girls on the boat, a

supreme sacrifice by Brina to leave home and to travel with her younger sister. They did it; they decided to get away and start in a new place. Did their parents know about this, did the family withdraw their support?

storing memories

It wasn't a catastrophe. The two girls, sisters, held onto their memories of family at home, and they replicated the best parts in a new and disordered place.

Because records are kept in this way, I have only the name of the father of Abraham and Brina and Hannah and Esther Israel.

Samson Israel. Furniture Broker.
Residence: 7 Constitution Row, Gray's Inn Road.

Elsewhere, in other papers, it is named as Gray's Inn Lane. I have found it on the map of London, seen it noted as a current address of the Open University. In these records I am given, in its flourishing script, the Hebrew names of all of the children. Born between 1831 and 1836. Mother nowhere named.

And then they embarked on a journey and travelled to another part of the world when they were still adolescents. Along with all of those other young women and children and older women, too, spinsters sturdy or broken down. Emigrants escaping the dead end of poverty, overcrowding, lack of sunshine. Their passage subsidised, they are special free settlers, the original ten-pound Poms. The Highland and Emigrants Society was established in 1851 and within two years had sent three thousand assisted emigrants to Australia. The society offered a new chance at life in Canada or Australia to people who they said could no longer be supported by their country, their overcrowded and wet little island.

There are historical records of the voyage of the *Travancore* but the generalisations don't fit. The dominant group holds the focus, the Irish and English girls setting off to make good in a new place. Building on a chance to do well in life and escape hardships. The Israel sisters' name is misspelt as Grael on the Certificate of Final Departure, but this is the problem with handwritten records. They are listed alongside families named Morris and Love and Buchanan and Beckett and Langsford.

The very nature of a colony a million miles from anywhere else gives an impression of it as a refuge, a hiding place for people escaping something somewhere else. For generations Perth girls have been told by parents, and probably sensible aunts, to beware of men from the East or even further afield. To avoid confidence men, strangers to this home town. Such men must be escaping a past to want to come this far, to a place where they don't belong. You can take this idea right back to the first white settlers: certainly the convicts didn't have much of a choice, but those who stayed, once given their ticket-of-leave, often didn't allow wives and children back in England to follow them out here, despite the assistance provided by the authorities in the interests of family values.

Miraculously, there are shipboard diaries and accounts by working-class people of the journey from England to Australia in the middle of the nineteenth century. They lie in libraries and have been transcribed into books. Here is a genre to work within, a model. I want to know the lives of Brina and Esther and the only way possible is through words, so I write a fictional account of a sea journey lasting one hundred and six days and include these two young women, my ancestors.

Going By The Travancore
From Plymouth on the 30th September 1852
Brina and Esther Israel
May God Preserve
Them and
Keep Us From Evil

Journal of Brina Israel, a passenger on the *Travancore,* who was born on the 15th April 1833 and is emigrating today to Australia with her sister Esther in search of a new life for both of us. We are the daughters of Samson Israel and Rachael Israel of Gray's Inn Lane, London, and the sisters of Abraham and Hannah Israel. I have never kept a journal before but I can write well. I have only one book to take on my journey to read, the *Saturday Magazine.*

30 Sept Weighed anchor at half past four and set sail at six o'clock. This is the start of an adventure to our New World. A sad journey, leaving our own life behind. Father still did not know when we joined the ship about Esther's baby. We have spared him and Abraham the shame of her mistake. And broken his heart that we have gone so far away for our new home. Will we ever see them again? I don't think we can. It is for me to protect Esther now and make our chances in Australia. I will admit to some fear about what is before me. I do not know honestly what I will find in this new country. And with a baby to care for too! It has been a long time since I held a baby and cared for it. I do not know enough about this country Australia.

1 Oct We were all rather ill last night on our first night at sea. We are living in a dormitory with bunks side by side and Esther and I sharing one. Lucky we are both short in body, but her tummy poked into our bed largely I can say. No privacy for us, just curtains in front of our beds and then our eating tables in the middle space. The bunks and all of the space is easily made dirty — in fact it was already a mess and smelly when we first came on board. It's all very cramped and close so you can hear everything happening in the beds. The sound of the ship's timbers which I first mistook in my sleep for a dying cat is now a great relief because it covers over some other dreadful sounds. There is yelling at night and snoring and people being sick and children crying. Esther was terribly ill all night. I hope she will calm down soon because today she is still looking pale and suffering so. The water closets are few and very uncomfortable. Usually the portholes are left open and when sometimes you are sitting there a great gush of wind and then water will come in and knock you.

We are all the single women together. With the single men at the front of the ship and the married people between us. Already I can see that the Captain and Matron and other working people see it as their duty to keep the men and girls apart. They guard us like hawks and don't let us even talk to the men. What would happen if we did? No one can tell yet that Esther is carrying child. She has hidden this so well for all of these months.

We have to carry our food across the whole length of the ship from where it has been cooked and then eat it in our bunk area, so you can imagine it has lost its appeal by that time when it is cold and you have been looking at it in a long queue of girls.

We have heard about some terrible things on other ships to Australia — about fights between men for one girl, about the favours promised by captains and sailors to girls, about what is available once we arrive in Fremantle, about jobs and how the men can make it easier. I just want to get there and have Esther's baby born without a fuss.

Dear Mother
I am already sad to be leaving you and Father and Abraham and dear Hannah and we have had only three nights away from home and My Own Dear Family. Setting out on this long journey makes me afraid — I don't know what we are going to. What if we don't like Australia, or we cannot get work? I am afraid that it will be frightful, full of brutes. Already the girls on this boat are rougher than me and Esther. Irish girls who have to fight hard about everything. They are poor things, afraid too and showing it by protesting about everything. Some of these girls have been fighting each other at night. I'm not sure where they get the spirits for it. We are suffering, or mostly Esther is, with our seasickness and it is so hard there is never any rest from that rocking and the smells all held down together. The water closets are few and because they are connected to the outside of the boat it means that when the sea is rough water comes back in through the pipes and drenches the poor user of the convenience. Some big swells send water right through the underdeck, wetting everything.

Please send my love and Esther's to everyone. I will keep writing over the journey and then send these letters to you when we reach Fremantle. It will be sad to be apart from you on your birthday, but I will be thinking always of my Dear Family and wishing you well.

With fond love Brina.

10 Oct Things have been terrible for us on this boat with Esther's sickness. I finally had to tell the Surgeon that she was carrying child because she was too scared to. He had already known this he said but there was nothing to be done for her. The diarrhoea started two days ago after she ate some probably spoiled meat, her first meal for days. The Surgeon gave her the chalk treatment and it had certainly stopped the problem and bound her up. He tells us that she is more than seven months gone and will in all likelihood deliver her baby before we arrive in Fremantle. I suppose I always knew that but was hoping that the timing might be different, that we could get to our destination first. My poor little sister is so afraid of this event and, I suppose I must admit, so am I.

1 Nov We crossed the line today and the whole ship became a happier place, even if only for a day. A strange idea to go over such a line, an equator. Some of the sailors went to much trouble to put on an entertainment for us, and everyone made such a fuss of cheering us into our new world. We are all now different!

Soon enough, I realised, I had stopped looking at our landscape of sea and sky and our progress which is after all so hard to measure. I use the sea and the sky now to project all of my ideas about Fremantle and Perth from what I have been told and what we were told in London. There are different stories and I spend the day staring into the blue and green and picturing us. That is what makes me feel calm which is a funny thing. But if I imagine buildings and horses and open spaces, and not really wanting to see many of these girls and ladies again, then I am curiously free of all that surrounds me like waiting a long time to use a water closet or trying to write in a straight line into this journal.

10 Nov Some terrible things have happened on this ship. Yesterday a man threw himself off the poop deck straight into the ocean. He had been losing his mind, howling all day and yelling at night. He fought off the Surgeon until finally he gave up and then yesterday, after causing trouble for a week, he jumped. He had a wife and three children and I think they felt safer after he had died but the poor little bedraggled heap sat and wept for the rest of the day. They couldn't take any help from anyone.

I can't keep up this journal properly. There is too much to do and worry about without taking the time to write it down. Esther is doing much better but there have been bad times and I'm sure there will be more. We had a frightening storm and I was not sure we would escape its fury. We are so flimsy against this force. By day the sea is a fierce and remarkable thing. I have not ever seen anything like it. I wish that I could describe its beauty, its colour. It is vast and all we have. Each day passes with lots of talking to my sister, in gentle words, and receiving advice we didn't ask for from goodly ladies who have also had babies. It was helpful at first, but then they all say different things and give their terrible stories. Each one speaks as if she invented having a baby.

20 Nov Yesterday, Esther bore her baby. The labour was long and hard — it started in the afternoon of the day before, and we were certainly the spectacle of the ship being how noisy and pained she was. The baby was born in a little distress but by this evening she has more or less settled. Oh, the scorching redness of the act. It is not what I expected. It was terrible and then when that little body finally came out of Esther's body all that was ugly dissolved. Esther is very sore and she is aching all over. She bled a lot, but the Surgeon is sure she will improve quickly. I held this little thing we have named Emma Alice and made my prayers that we will all be kept safe, three of us now, as we arrive at Fremantle. It is such a miraculous thing, that baby inside little Esther, forming from her own flesh, and then coming to greet us, a new Israel.

12 Jan We have been told we are close to Fremantle. The

land is jagged and solid. It is a different colour than I was expecting. I am full of trepidation about where we will go. How all of these girls and women will fare is an unknown idea to me. So many of them without a single sensible moment in a long day. I can already feel how hot the sun is that beats down onto us. I am very tired — babies are demanding creatures and being on a crowded ship is not the best place for it. Esther is happy to be saying goodbye to this as her home. Some of the ladies on board have been very generous in assisting us with Emma Alice. So has the Surgeon. He asks us how we will manage as single girls and tells us how to arrange some help in the town. There is a place we can stay, he told us, at least for the first few nights. I don't think, now that we are so close to our destination, that we will ever see England again.

My hair has grown some five inches since we left England. It must be all the fresh air and the worry. I am also much thinner than I was at home. The food has been of the poorest standard.

love

What sort of a man was he — the one Brina met and had babies with? Theodore Krakouer. She was twenty, he was thirty something, already married, the father of one. A convict with a wife and son safely back in the Mother Country. He had books delivered to him while he was at Portland Prison in England. He was a reader, and a record was kept of what he borrowed. The books and magazines he selected had the following titles: *Saturday Magazine, Cottage Visitor, Caves of the Earth, The Snow Storm, History of the Plague*. Does this evidence mean that he had an imagination, an interest in the natural world, the damage that men could do to each other, the ferocity of disease?

I yearn to give Brina the access she needs to read and borrow books in Perth. The idea of knowledge and learning is so central to her faith: the book stands at the centre of its inquiring spirit. In all of her years in Perth and Fremantle it is likely that she didn't get to read books. There were readings from William Shakespeare at the Fremantle Literary Institute from 1868 onwards; they were hardly years when she could have attended, with nine children in her care. She might not have been allowed into such an institute anyway, as ex-convicts were barred for decades and she was likely tainted with the same brush.[23]

Brina and her sister Esther both married Jews in Fremantle: convicts, enterprising men who made money, who started up crazy schemes.[24] "Married" is the genteel way of putting it, because they didn't use the State and its laws to formalise their couplings. The details are sketchy: Elias Lapidus, Esther's man, traded and shipped horses to Singapore for the British Army. He was caught up in a shonky deal in Singapore and never returned. The idea of horses on boats amuses me.

I have ridden horses in the sea, watched them on the back of vehicles. Their bodies are beautiful, but not easily transported. The idea of a convict returning to the high seas so soon after his recent journey is intriguing, too. Theodore Krakouer, a willing and hard-working man, was a teamster, a general dealer. There are wild sightings of him I have found in books about heroic pioneering enterprises as a six-foot-eight-inch Russian on the Goldfields, a grand figure out of place after his convict papers told a different story, recording a much more modest height, a full twelve inches shorter. It appeared he worked his team of horses hard on the Williams Road. And then he went mad.

How were these two attracted? In the same way I am when the right person comes along, through a sharing of interests or a current of lust and intrigue? Or, bluntly, was it the requirement for living in a society, a satisfying of the urges of comfort and bodily needs? Was coupling necessary, a survival strategy? All of this attention to coupling in books about colonies and communities everywhere, in the past and the present. Information of unions, of entwining families and blood. The way that the progression of life is captured. It must have been important, even crucial, for Brina and Esther to find men to be with when they arrived at their destination. This was a brutal colony: the streets running with alcohol and urine and money, almost out of control, named an anarchic backwater.

Where did these lovers meet? Do they pretend to themselves that they are properly married? Do they practise a private Jewish ritual of expunging the first wife and replacing her? Being a bigamist so far from home isn't a risky venture anyway. They never married legally, according to the records.

Later on, when she is forty-seven years old, she marries finally under the law of the State. Her first legal marriage happens a long way from home, in Adelaide. They travel to Adelaide, return to Perth, and then they live happily ever after. It is three years since Theodore died. Perhaps they met on the streets of Fremantle with her brood of children. He had not been married before.

They were a married couple for the next twenty-two years. She died in 1902, on 8 November, at the age of sixty-nine in a hospital around the corner from where I live, in Fitzgerald Street, Perth. It was a cerebral haemorrhage and her illness had lasted for ten days. Her father's name is listed on the certificate as Abraham, which was the name of her firstborn. Rabbi David Freedman performed the rites and she was buried in the Jewish Orthodox section of Karrakatta Cemetery the following day.

Before that, though, returning to Perth after the wedding and honeymoon, they walk around the streets in amazement that they could feel so happy or contented in their lives. If they didn't feel this optimism, then why did they bother marrying so late? Brina and James Mardon.

Falling in love in the heat, in the harshness of the midday sun. Where can you sleep together, find some respite; hot and hard surfaces and the rough clothes covering your bodies. Sweaty friction of limbs and torsos and genitals. This ordeal of love. The imprints of intimacies carried on our bodies: palimpsests. When I look at her I can see the hands of all of her lovers, and all of those who tried.

There are people in the streets. A bustle of happiness. We go to Mount Eliza for the Sunday and we look down onto the river and we can see across to the banks on the other side. Everywhere the grasses are burnt by the sun. It is hot. So different from where I once came from, that crowded city of people and purpose. Over there my people are sleeping in their graves and even here my boy Sampson is dead before me. And my Theodore. I am happy now but I still carry Theo in my life — he is chained to me in his despair. The first man I loved and there it was. A hard life, and then it was ended. The father of my children.

Walking around Mount Eliza, the thick bush, this stillness. Well, there is noise in the air, an alarming penetration every now and then from the Rifle Shooting Club and then the bird calls that come after.

I will never forget, not even in my happiness now, how hard it was to find help in this colony when we needed it. Theodore was a Convict so they should have looked after him when he was sick. He was ruined by their system, from working in too much harsh sun and drinking too many spirits at the end of it. He didn't choose to come here and he worked like a bullock. I can't help but think about my boy Abraham and the troubles he has presently. He is somehow ruined by too much responsibility too early. He is greedy for pleasures, an unreliable husband. He is not happy for me to have a new husband.

But look at this wide clear meandering river, shining in the afternoon sun. We are on top of the world and we are happy. We are together.

comfort

When Brina and Esther first arrived in the colony, there was a shortage of accommodation and a crisis of oversupply of domestics after a critical time of not enough people or interest in this place to even sustain it. This colony was so badly organised it was falling apart, despite every lofty proclamation. They had got it wrong, often, its architects and developers; the result was a community of about five thousand white people teetering on the edge of collapse for decades. The ideals not properly implemented; the agriculture unsustainable; and the labour force insufficient. The colony needed slave labour to live, and so the convicts began to arrive in 1850, twenty-one years after the ideals and the purity of this colony were first discussed. But there are always two sides to every story and the same month that the colony finally decided to ask for convict labour, the British government:

> saw the passing of an Order-in-Council constituting Western Australia a fully fledged penal settlement. But the normal practice of publishing this order in Hansard was suspended by Lord Grey because the Governor and Council of Western Australia had yet to be informed. The British government was in fact in the process of deceiving the colony in an attempt to relieve a growing problem within Britain [after cessation of transportation to New South Wales in 1840].[25]

The opportunism of the colony, selecting what it needed in the form of human traffic and filling in gaps with people. They asked for a better class of convict, only petty criminals and professional failures. Then they called to liberate poor Irish and English girls from their squalor but remained selective about religion. The impossibility of accepting a Catholic girl into so many families to do domestic duties.

Where did these young women stay, before they began living with their two Jewish convicts, ticket-of-leave men who worked a livery stable in Fremantle? Where did they sleep on their first night? They arrived with two hundred others: domestics, prostitutes, wives, some with children, to service the colony, on the bride ship, the *Travancore*. When they arrived, was there a round-up point, a home for strays and waifs, a bed for those first few nights or weeks? Or did they live on the streets? There was temporary accommodation available in Goderich Street — an all-purpose building that had held female lunatics and was now the poorhouse — an immigrant depot and a servants' home but there might not have been room, given the number of arrivals on that day.

First stop, Fremantle. Before the big passenger terminal was constructed for the port of Fremantle in the 1960s, there was a corrugated tin shed, a big one, to house all of the services for the people arriving: customs, immigration, public toilets. In 1959, when my friend arrived with her young family from England to take up an academic post, this shed was daubed with a sign of welcome: POMS GO HOME. Within a couple of years, the ostentatious terminal was completed and capable of receiving thousands of people at one time, both passengers and those there to greet them. And before long, when people gave up ocean travel for faster and cheaper aeroplanes, the terminal was surplus to any need of the authorities. Now we travel to Fremantle to listen to music in the old terminal, the last time to hear Nick Cave and the Bad Seeds. When enough people dance on that expanse of parquetry flooring, it begins to feel like a trampoline. The dangerous dance of a huge crowd of people. We are going nowhere, right on the edge of the water. It is always too hot inside, so we sit out along that edge, and if we are lucky dolphins come right in and play and splash us and wet our beers.

Second stop, a bed for the night. I imagine myself lowering my head onto pillows in houses that are not my own. There is this obsession I have with other people's homes, staying in them, and imagining what life is like for them in that private space, what happens there. I usually get it wrong. The legacy of having lived alone for too many years. There is an image I have carried with me for years, a potent one. Of a silhouette in the hallway of a darkened house in the middle of the day, a winterish day, a good day to spend in front of the television with a blanket and pillows on the couch, or in bed with a lover. But on this Sunday I am walking the streets, exercising, and this is what I see. A woman in the house, a ghostly apparition. The gap of window, bare, across the front door of the terraced house. I am innocent, outside, uninvolved, have never seen her before. I glimpse her naked body, through that window, in that front bedroom. I cannot tell if she is moving in ecstasy or pain, whether it is fear that she is moving to or from. I also recognise elements of the gestures she uses — I have seen myself do them. In a mirror, or just in my mind's eye? I wonder, and feel confused.

I am circling around fantasy and what I know, both

from the present and the past. Open to persuasion, to changing my mind, to imaginings, to seeing the world in entirely new ways.

It is this fleeting image that comes to me when I think of the first steps of those girls on 13 January 1853, when they disembarked at Fremantle after a journey over the high seas for nearly four months. Making a picture of all the scariest images of Wild West towns and outposts I have seen in films, hot and as dry as hell. And then the intimacy and comfort of an interior space, a home, a bedroom. Did the baby wait to enter the world in the Swan River Colony, or did they disembark with it? There are no medical records and no surgeon's journals of that voyage and so I can only speculate.

Brina's first baby, Abraham, was born at Fremantle in 1853 when she was twenty. Claimed in the State Archives as the first Hebrew born in Western Australia, this is the thrall of family myth-making: the first of everything, an assertion of supremacy, we came, we conquered. That is why every family of lengthy occupation has a firstborn story, tailor-made for district or nationality. It makes us feel special.

The mother of the first Hebrew baby wrote to the Melbourne Hebrew Congregation for assistance after she had given birth seven times. Her sister Esther was living in Sydney, married to a man named James Sargent and mother of their children, William,

Catherine, Augustus, the three who followed Emma Alice. I have to make up a letter to fit because the records have not been kept.[26]

> Dear Sirs
> I write from Fremantle and implore you to help me. We do not as yet have a Congregation here — we are a small group of families trying to get on as best we can. I arrived more than ten years ago with my sister Esther from London. She is now a member of the Sydney Congregation. I bore my husband sons and daughters. Although it has been difficult to maintain our rituals in this foreign place, we have made every effort to do so. I ask your assistance regarding the circumcision of my sons. My first son Abraham, the first Hebrew baby born in this colony, was duly circumcised when a Rabbi made a visit to Fremantle. But my other sons remain uncircumcised and I see no hope of us being able to arrange so important a ritual for them as their commitment to life and faith.
>
> I am your obedient servant
> Mrs Krakouer

the battles

Firstly, her husband went mad. She kept going, she worked harder than ever before. There were now ten of them in the house, a little limestone cottage in

Fremantle. Sometimes it felt like they were sinking into the mire, or the cesspit. It was chaotic, but each of them got on with living. They had a productive energy. No more babies; that was one benefit of Theo's distractions and illness over these past years. All credit must go to her, say the people of Fremantle, for maintaining the business and for training Abe to be such a competent business proprietor. They worked well together; they ran the business with a firm hand. Suppliers, customers, drivers all knew this and respected Mrs Krakouer. Any increase in profits, any rewards, were due to her hard work and they flowed through to make life better for her large family.

She wished her sister was still living in Fremantle because she craved the company and the way that they had shared their experiences. It didn't matter that she was spurned by some of the citizens of Fremantle: the toffs and those who thought her husband a disgrace. If the Sampsons were too good for her, then she knew that she was a good and righteous woman, that she maintained her faith and that was enough. Many things had been difficult, but she appreciated her life.

Her problems are recorded in a series of letters. I found them in the microfiche archive of the State of Western Australia. I didn't know before I found them if she was a literate woman, an articulate woman who could hold her rights and allow them to inform her argument. She writes letters with her reasonably neat hand to the man holding the highest office in the colony. He arranges for reviews of her capacity to pay to keep Theodore, her poor mad husband, in the asylum. They keep stating that she is a shrewd dealing woman, that she does very good business but will gladly shuck her responsibilities if given half a chance.

They had Abraham sign a paper to say we would pay for the maintenance of Theodore while he gets better in there. It isn't long before they start to pressure us and ask questions around the town. Then they make a picture out of this mess of lies and half-truths. That there are only two children at home and not nine, that my baby David is a girl, that we are flowing with money. These fools have no idea what it costs to feed children and horses and men who drive our dray when Abe is on another job. A good business! But it costs money to keep it going — that is what they don't understand when they have budgets from England and a wage every week.

This is the list of my crimes:
I am a shrewd dealing person and so is my son Abraham.
I lease a piece of land, I build a house to be used as a store and so of course I can give more money to anyone needing it.
The two good teams on the road between Williams and Perth.
The credit is so good in Fremantle that if I wanted anything to my heart's content I could have it — up to the value of one thousand pounds!

DON'T THESE PEOPLE KNOW WHAT BUSINESS IS?

Your most obedient servant
My most obedient slave
I will give you all my money — how is that?
(An obedient mule)

~

The family is in turmoil. They are trying to force my hand. I cannot feed and clothe another baby, a grown baby who is also a madman. I write these letters and wait and wait for a reply, for some resolution. Everything takes so long in this place and the talk takes over in the streets. They all feel sorry for me, more is the pity, but they seem to hate me for all else. That I am busy and capable, that I can speak up for myself. Getting Theodore locked up was the hardest thing I did. I didn't want him hurt because he is harmless and has lost his mind. He never hurt his family. When I was with him in the bush, just before all of this, he left me and was lost four days and nights without food or drink and I gave notice to a police constable and when he was found I sent him to Fremantle with my son. The Doctors then gave my son certificates to get him in the Asylum which cost us three guineas.

Every one of these steps takes from our purse, makes a hardship of the next day. Why is this business not easier? Why is it that the Doctors cannot just see that the man is in distress and help him? He spooks the children with his presence.

He was kept in for a few weeks while I was in the country

and then the doctors discharged him. He was not out of the Asylum one hour before a great many people could see he was worse than ever. My daughter was in charge of the housekeeping and, frightened, made an application to Mr Slade and to Dr Barnett. They of course could do nothing for him unless she paid again for certificates which of course she could not do. Mr Slade told her if he committed himself in any way he would be taken in which of course he did in the following way.

He went into the house of a woman who I think could not be of very good character and he sent for beer for her she would not give him any change of the money he gave her so he took two common tumblers and told her he would summons her for the rest. He brought them away openly in the daytime and when the constable came for him he told him the same as he told others. My daughter wishing him some comfort and her some peace advised him to go to the station house. He then told Mr Slade he would not be tried by him so Mr S committed him for trial and he has been in the Lunatic Asylum ever since. I am sorry to say worse than ever. The Doctors can testify to that.

The Sister was being summoned to attend the sessions against him. I think it is a great pity that he should be took to Perth in his present state and myself with such a large helpless family to support. I wish to spare all the expenses I can and this is why I continue to send my pleading letters which make me feel like a compromised person. I hate your rules and your lack of assistance. All of this begging for a favourable answer as soon as is convenient to you makes me hate myself. Begging your pardon for troubling you.

Begging your pardon for troubling you. I am very sorry but I am also so angry I am at the point of explosion. I have so much to think about and my house is sinking and these children are worried and my husband as you are aware is now a Lunatic in the Asylum. So I am alone and I left with a large and helpless family to support.

The husband smells of fear and of sickness. He is a wreck. He is wrecked by too much sun, too much drink, too much hard work. I am next. I am doing this alone with only the assistance of my eldest son a Lad of 20 years of age. He is trying his best to keep us all out of the Poor House and I hope with God Almighty's help to be able to keep out of it.

I have already been there twice and that is quite sufficient for me.

~

My husband suffered a great deal of unnecessary trouble as you are well aware. God forbid I should say it was that brought him where he is. I should not trouble you with this only I am afraid my son and myself will be affected in the same manner. I FEAR WE TOO WILL GO MAD. WATCH US.

He was committed for trial to be tried in January they have now sent me a bill for his keep in the Lunatic Asylum on the

1st of September to the 31st of December for which of course there is no claim. There is only one thing I have to ask you that is begging that my Husband becomes a free inmate of the Asylum.

In fact it would be trespassing too much on your valuable time in telling you how I am served there is one thing favourable in the public sympathy within my truly unfortunate position and I can only trust that you will do the same and you will find that I will never transgress the Law.

I only want fair play.

I would be very glad if you allow me to see you at any time or would think proper to me I would not trouble you only I am duty bound according to my own conscience and the advice of my friends to contradict such a base falsehood that has been told to you and I think I ought to know the author of such an untruth. What I write to you the inhabitants of Fremantle can prove. I only wish the person that gave you the information would take my ample means and support my Husband and my self and children. I would be truly grateful and so would my Husband's creditors for there is a good many of them in this place. When my Husband was first put into the Asylum the bailiff immediately afterwards came in to the house.

~

When will you answer my letters? These are letters with information and requests; they are written according to the rules and they all make sense. They are written in good English, as good as yours, your High and Mighty. How long will it take you to read them and reply? Sending out letters into thin air and this is now a matter of the utmost urgency and import. Where are you?

~

The Husband owes a great deal of money which can be provided. I am paying them all a little at the time on purpose to keep my few belongings together to enable my son and myself to try and get a living for ourselves without becoming a burden upon government. The public know the unnecessary trouble my poor Husband was often put to. No wonder that he ends his days in a Lunatic Asylum. I am afraid that my son will be driven there too unless I have the means to send him out of the Colony and then perhaps government will be kind enough to keep my children and me for already one of Krakouer's creditors not satisfied to wait has sent a summons to the Lunatic asylum. Poor fellow they won't let him rest there. I would feel obliged if you would grant me an interview as I wish to speak to you. Please name the time that will suit your convenience.
I am Yours obediently.

~

This is the last letter I will write to the bastards. If I don't hear now I will leave the colony as soon as I can. I can scarcely express my feelings when unfortunately I have to mention the circumstances connected with my Husband now in the Lunatic Asylum. I have been applied to pay for the keep of my Husband a sum now which unfortunately to say is not in my power to pay. How willing I should have been to do so had I not been left with a large helpless family and the only dependence I have is in my eldest son a lad of twenty years of age who has to work very hard to support us. (Most people say great credit is due to him.) Too much put on him must be the cause of him wishing to leave the colony.

He my son is willing or am I if we can get some assistance from government to send my Husband home to his native country to his relatives in Berlin for the present it is as much as we can do to keep out of the poor House — should business prosper I should only be too happy to offer the support of my Husband — at present I must beg the release of any payment demanded of me and my son. I therefore hope and pray Sir you will be good enough to intercede on my behalf and I will be ever grateful. I am now living in Perth and if you will allow me the honour of an interview with you I will explain more fully to you how I am situated and will give you ample proofs if required.
Your very humble and obedient servant,
(I am humble and I am your servant. Isn't that enough for you?)
I am desperate, I am getting sick. Help me. Please.

Theodore died in the asylum on 18 May 1877; it is not clear who paid for his keep as a *Lunatic* for those four years.

Brina's death

At the end of all of my research, my attempts to be methodical, and creative, the process is turned on its head when I find a most important piece of information by sheer good luck. I discover Brina *after* Theodore's death, rescue her from obscurity. I find my old great-great-grandmother.

It came in a hint from a silly old man about a burial site and was followed up by the work of a genealogist, but didn't even require her highly skilled work. From the records of burials, she ran a search on the name Brina and found her. We had begun to think she might have died in another part of Australia or even back in England, but there she was in Karrakatta Cemetery. That was the key to the end of Brina's life, as there were no people around to ask about her fate, and the rest of her life.

At the age of forty-seven, in 1880, Brina Israel, Widow, travelled to Adelaide to marry Joseph Lucas Mardon, forty-four, a Bachelor and Sawyer from Mahogany Creek, a village in the hills outside Perth. Their witnesses were Ann Griffith, Matron, and Minnie Hoskins, Spinster, both of Adelaide, and the place in which they celebrated was the Office of Registrar General in Victoria Square. Brina's handwriting, judging by her signature, had hardened since the last decade, with many bold straight lines. She calls herself

Krakouer and each *k* is very sharp. The way that I approach handwritten historical records is always cautious, but at first I note his occupation as lawyer and think, happily, that Brina's fortunes had improved in her second marriage. She might not have had to work as hard in her advancing years. Mr and Mrs James Mardon returned to Perth to live after their wedding.

a curve of shadows

The shame of being far from home can lead to questions of how you found yourself transplanted somewhere else. A pattern initiated from the start: exile as a way of hiding away from what you fear. To be a convict was an enforced exile, a body transported for purposes not your own. But for the rest of us who follow the convict there is an ostensible choice of exile or acceptance. The terms of acceptance are not as simple as might at first appear; loneliness is at the centre of it and forces the point one way or the other.

A curve of shadows across a life leads to a store of bitter sentiment. We don't know how to go on. I uncover the picture of family and, while it is better to know the details, they won't save me from anything. This is the underbelly to communion and family knowledge. I wanted to write this family story through the metaphor of archaeology: I wanted to dig and find my evidence through the flints and the scrappy information in front of me, to find what was available. Developing a scientific hypothesis, and living with distrust: knowing that everyone who opposed me could easily take issue with any findings. Using a popular metaphor for writing, this archaeology, this digging and uncovering and sifting. I found a family of individuals, many of whom had chosen exile and continued to live in Perth.

The shame piles up. And sits there in a heap, stinking. It isn't dealt with, isn't discussed, turns into the family's jewels. The list of words becoming compost: the convict is syphilitic, and so is at least one of his sons. A criminal, he goes mad, dies of it all — the softening of the brain also called Tabes Dorsalis, *the cause of death of his youngest son. Men and women have sexual congress even when it is not allowed. Babies are born out of wedlock, adopted; some of them are taken away because under the policies of the government of the day they are half-caste. Nobody talks about any of this.*

a voice in the belly

Borough
Of
Portsmouth

The Jurors for our Lady the Queen upon their oath present that Carl Dollman *per se* Guilty late of the Parish of Portsea within the Borough of Portsea with the Borough of Portsmouth Labourer and **Teoder Kiakauer** late of the same place Labourer on the twenty third day of October in the year of our Lord one thousand eight hundred and forty eight **with force and arms** at the Parish aforesaid in the Borough aforesaid three silk dresses at the value of four pounds and ten shillings, two satin dresses of the value of six pounds, two pieces of muslin delaine of the value of twenty three shillings, four shawls of the value of five pounds, five yards of woollen

plaid at the value of thirty shillings, two scarves at the value of twenty shillings, one silk visile at the value of twenty five shillings, four petticoats of the value of eight shillings, three shifts of the value of five shillings, three table cloths of the value of six shillings, five yards of table cloths linen of the value of seven shillings and four sheets of the value of six shillings of the Goods and Chattels of Henry Seeling, in the dwelling house of the said Henry Seeling there situate, then and there being found then and there in the said dwelling house feloniously did steal take and carry away against the form of the Statute in such case made and provided and against the peace of our Lady the Queen her Crown and Dignity.
Howard
To be each transported for the term — 15 years.[27]

Fremantle

To begin in the one room: its four solid walls, the amazing height to the ceiling, the dimensions and the grace of this corner room. The room looks out onto a peaceful garden, a cultivated native garden, and from its windows you can also see, if you bring a chair into the room and stand on it, the features of the city of Fremantle.

I have spent time in this room, many hours on end, always following the pursuits of what I could grandly call the life of the mind: all of my passions. Writing and talking about writing. Thinking about how things are made in the world. This must be where I first came to think about Theodore Krakouer, my grandmother's grandfather, and the end of his days in the Swan River Colony. Started to imagine him as an imprisoned body in this asylum for lunatics built by convict labour in 1861 and now used as an arts centre. At first with no idea what it might mean to discover a madman in the family. Was it an incorrect diagnosis? Are there concerns about genetic inheritances? What is this deep shame? This man stole satin dresses and fabrics with arms and force, was sentenced to fifteen years' hard labour and sent to Australia when the convict era had almost finished. And died of syphilis and exhaustion at the end of a short life. That room was where my research began. The first artefacts found were two letters and a certificate. The first is dated 30 August 1873 and states simply that Theodore Krakouer was admitted as a patient to the Fremantle Asylum and that his son Abraham has agreed to pay for the maintenance of the patient during the time of his confinement. It is signed by H C Barnett, Medical Practitioner of Fremantle. The second is dated 24 September, twenty-five days later when Barnett, after careful examination, discharges Theodore on the basis of a successful convalescence. This is when he really goes berserk because it is only a matter of two weeks before he is a certified lunatic. He rampages through the streets of Fremantle.

CERTIFICATE OF LUNACY

I, the undersigned, H. C. Barnett of Fremantle in the Colony of Western Australia, a medical practitioner of the said colony, and now in actual practice, hereby certify that I on the 10th day of October at Fremantle in the said colony personally examined Theodore Krakouer of Fremantle and that the said Theodore Krakouer is a Lunatic and a proper person to be taken charge of and detained under care and treatment, and that I have focused this opinion on the following grounds.

1st Facts indicating insanity and found by myself: Delusion. Says he hears a voice operating from his belly giving

him messages from God
Almighty to destroy the world.

2nd Other facts indicating
insanity communicated to me
by other/s:
Has been drinking since he left
the Asylum and is in a state of
delusional excitement.

H. C. Barnett.

I applied for, and was granted, permission to look through the records kept for state mental health authorities since the middle of last century. If you can prove familial links you are entitled to search through records, which have been kept in a fairly haphazard manner.

Preparing myself for sadness, I investigated Surgeon's Day Journals, Case Books and Admission Books from 1857 to 1896. But all I found in the banality of official record keeping were two entries about Theodore: his admittance and the announcement of his death. I think it was just bad luck that there was so little evidence: some books had gone missing, others had probably been destroyed. There were names named; the community of lunatics, Theodore's fellow patients, were detailed. Who made a repeat visit, why they were there. The surveilling eye of authority watched out for offences such as masturbation, sallow complexions, and the pulling out of one's own hair. It is, of course, such detail that is easily noticed when you pore through documents like these. As are the cases of post-partum distress and depression. Supposed causes of insanity included masturbation, failed love affairs, lactation, opium, religion, and sunstroke. They put hot bottles to the feet of those suffering, and made wild judgements daily. "He has had 73 fits in the last 7 days. His intelligence is now much the same as it was prior to the seizures." "He does as little as he can." "He is wild, excitable." "He soiled himself and had other filthy practices."[28] They gave Theodore daily rations of tobacco, along with two ounces of brandy and one pint of beef tea.

In his first year locked up the average daily muster was thirty-seven. Lunacy had not been a big problem, or not named as such anyway, until 1857 when seven or eight prisoners were so afflicted and the authorities at a loss to know how to dispose of them. They considered a section of the old prison in Perth town at that time, but soon moved on to the idea of an asylum, purpose-built. They were anticipating problems in the colony, preparing for the future. In that year, the *Perth Gazette* wrote: "God help the poor madmen for in Western Australia they have none other to help them."[29]

his voice

I am ghost-trading. Theodore's body in the dormitory dreaming of other times, dreaming of his life. A sleeping body, a mound on a mattress under a regulation blanket. There isn't much body left, only a skinny thing, not so much emaciated as worn down. The mound is child-size, but the length of his body is still there, five feet eight. He is going mad here and that is why he is hiding.

He stands up and moves away from the bed. His walk is like a dance in slow motion: he needs to find a balance and he does it in an elaborate sway, a complex signal system of four limbs. The head moving too, in counter rhythm to his body. *A straddling walk.*

If, out of respect for the dead and the still living, flesh and blood are banished in this account, and only the paths he took are shown, lines and paths and that is all, how will his journey be shaped? Will he look like a madman or a pioneer, a criminal or a father and grandfather? Ghosts must suffice; disembodied voices that spring from the belly. There are no other mementos or objects carried down, none that I have found, aside from court notices in newspapers and a Certificate of Lunacy. His crimes always clever and playful; my memorials made of the most precarious materials.

I was charged with a robbery by a diamond merchant and a

jeweller. If he had only been more patient he would have got his money in the normal way — goods for money. I spent so much time in court, locked up, all for the crime of swapping his diamond rings for my half-boiled potatoes. They imprisoned me and my cape, my great coats, my hundred weight of sponges. It was me and a bundle of my belongings, well-cut. Calling me Krakueri, Mister Charles, the German Jew. Or did I tell them that name? And once I had got them off my back, in Clerkenwell and Bristol, all over that infernal island, I am caught again and this time for stealing fine fabrics and laces. Sent to Australia as punishment for muslin delaine and woollen shawls. Yes, they are about equal.

My life has proceeded viciously. My mind shaped and locked itself against these brutalities until now I am a shell of a man without even a functioning mind. Moments of lucid thought and then I'm gone. There is nothing neutral about life. I am thinking of my parents in Cracow — this English you know is not my native tongue — and in their imagination Cracow was a haven, it was where we would rest at the end of our days. In the shtetl we were our community, autonomous, complete. And God saw the wickedness of man was great in the earth, and that every imagination of the thoughts of his heart was only evil continually. *And then we had to move, always moving, chased from beloved places when foreign powers meddle in how we will live. We go to Berlin. This burden of our race. How I ended my days in this place when I started there — the burden of our race. My midnight breathing, the only time I pause and am not hot. An infernal heat. Bright sun beating down all year. And that fierce ice wind at night through Fremantle town just to remind you between day and night, cold and hot. There is nothing in the middle. The bush like Palestine — covered in Spring by beautiful green of grass and herbs and then soon scorched brown and parched in the heat and drought of summer. But always cold at night. Now these are the names of the children of Israel, which came into Fremantle; every man and his household came with Theodore.*

Abraham, Phoebe, Rachael, Fanny, Sampson, Rudolph, Philip, Raphael, David.

And all of the souls that came out of the loins of Theodore were many souls and they also numbered Samuel back in London, my forgotten son. Seven sons and three daughters.

> There was a man in the land of Uz, whose name was Job; and that man was perfect and upright, and one that feared God, and eschewed evil. And there were born unto him seven sons and three daughters.

I look at the walls of limestone in this asylum, I sit and stare through long days. Think I have captured every detail, every rivulet, the cadence of a wall. And then after hours, days, months, I suddenly see a new feature. Seen entirely for the first time. A pattern in the limestone, its colour at the different times of the day. The same with the symmetry of the windows on the asylum's north-facing wall, all the way up to the tower. The way that they have been placed, the logic of the pattern. I look and look at these things, the things around me, and I do it for my own comfort and to stay in the world. Because when I can notice a perfectly new thing after habituation then I know my mind still works.

I WAS EDUCATED IN THE PUBLIC SCHOOL OF BERLIN. That is what I told them in a loud voice in England in gaol when I was asked everything about myself. They wouldn't know our words for education and schools. But I attended the Yeshiva in Berlin, and I studied the Talmud. My father struggled to support me and I was a devoted student for as long as I could be. We started early in the morning with prayers and used all of the day for studying the holy book. We students with the old men gathered around tables in the synagogue to ward off the melancholy of dusk. My study there didn't last long, but those lessons and that dedication to learning I have kept with me for all of these days since.

When as a boy I first attended classes at the kheyder, there was a feast. We believed in celebrations. The other students were invited. When I began to study the Five Books of Moses we also had a feast. So you see this is all before my bar mitzvah so it is true that we were a celebrating community. When my brother Solomon was born I was already in the kheyder and all of the boys came into the house and stood around his little body and they recited the prayers "Hear, O Israel" and "The Angel Who Redeems Me". They came every day and each time they were given a savour of sweetness until the baby was circumcised.[30]

And then we had another happy ceremony for that day. We also did this with the baby Abraham in Fremantle. We were able to because there was a Rabbi visiting from the Eastern colonies, but with all the other sons of mine it could not be done.

I remember perfectly, even now, where we lived before we began our infernal exile, the movement from the shtetl to Berlin, where I learnt to read and write, and alone with my brother across to London and then to my shame of being caught and locked in Millbank Prison and then Portland Prison for two years before I set sail to the New World. Ha! This looks just like another little England full of dreadful men following rules, but only with more sunshine and bush.

Our faith had such a beautiful shape. The sound of prayer and song, the holiness of the people mixed with their love. It was together — one and the same thing. I still recall an event that took place in our shtetl when I was a small boy. A cantor and his choir visited for the Sabbath. Although it was at the beginning of my life I have heard nothing as sweet since. We walked along the river when we left the synagogue and we were a family together. My mother wore a brooch with tiny pieces of precious glass. I pressed my child's face upon her wonderful bosom, always warm and welcoming of her sons, and the edges of the brooch made an imprint on my face.

"Bring, bring, bring peace, goodness, and blessing." It has been so much time passed since I felt like a righteous Jew.

On a summer's day and we are playing. The winter has been cold and very long and we are only now thawing out. The children play, stretching our limbs, laughing excitedly. It is muggy and we may see a storm tonight. The smell of orange blossom carries through the air. And the aromas of food from the kitchens of our houses. This is my lost world: I will never see anything like it again.

The only creature on the earth I never liked is the Matron of this Asylum. It is clear she was ruined by coming to this town of dogs. She must have been bitten. Now she is cruel and there are many stupid and foolish and harmless old men and women, halfwits, and they are very badly hurt by her. We all of us are still human and that is what they have stopped thinking of. Humans who are frail of mind or body and sometimes both. This cesspit is where we have all ended and some of us were pushed. There are not only Jews and dirty old beggars in here but some of the young men of the finest families of Perth and soon they too are dirty and whimpering. Hard done by from parents and then by the jailers in here. Cities are brutal but colonies can be worse, attracting failures and nasty creatures. Once I was lost in the bush after I travelled with Brina and it was hot and I was in a fever and everything was prickly and forbidding of comfort. Walking in circles for hours, for days, four days, crying for help or some dear woman to give me a drink. I was nearly perished. That was easier than coming face to face with Matron when she is in a mood or you need something or you have made a mess. I ask for my daily ration of tobacco and it is given to me. That is all I get apart from a flogging or being locked in a quiet and damp room. A dingly dell, a fine muddle I'm in now. This is the end of a long line of mess. Trickstering help I have given to those who were with me. I am the Rascal. On the road I hoed. Ha Ha! Friends and those beloved children and wives in this hellhole of life. I've seen the bad, yes, most of it has been right in here, though, inside me. Right in here and made by me. I have this reminder in my belly. The women have babies there and I have a voice, my talkative companion.

I've been bad and now I'm mad, sick and tired. The drink has got me fired right up. Breathed through my pores, done its magic grandly. And this other thing winding through my nerves. A sickness, a pox. I fly off the edge of things when I hear a sound not made by me. Don't talk to me if you aren't facing me you'll give me a fright and I might shock you too. We are as good as dead in this madhouse — they cannot help us now. I shocked some of those people in Fremantle town drinking. Took them all over the streets. Made a mess, stood my ground. Now I'm here without Brina a whingeing woman anyway. Most of the time disagreeable. And the children, only two I will miss will be the oldest and the youngest, Abe and little David. Abe will come if he can. The boy can't. Not allowed.

These things have made me cranky or crazy: being pushed out of home going to Berlin. Then it all changed. I'm my own creation. I know how many times I made myself over many times the way they believed that bad voice in the gaol. The doctor too and the way that it is there telling me all the time I lied about something and then it happened. Now it has taken me over. I have a pain across my eyes, a band around my head. Squeezing my head and squashing my brains. Makes me feel every move could be a dangerous one. It hurts. I'm tired already of all the stupid men in this place. The lunatics. The killers. These black and white birds making their sounds together like they're making babies. I never heard that sound before. Here it's always in the mornings. Early, before we are woken and made to dress and get into the dining slop room for their horrible food. I might have been a convict on that ship for week after week, but still this is the most horrible vile and sick food I have eaten. Remind me of the reasons to continue to live.

But what of love?

I know how to love. Human love, not the noise of those birds. I want to be loved. I'm good at it. Lovable, a loving man. I can be good at that. I'm soft — my mother and my father, that was love. And Jane and Samuel in London. Brina and Esther here. The sisters, two girls from London. And that first Fremantle baby, son of a bastard convict. A bastard himself. Abraham. No one sees me here. All I have are loonatics and ladies who contrive to make us, keep us, upright and good. In the garden clever in their fancy clothes. Full of it their luck. That we are here, so they can be there in goodness and grace. The good life in Perth and Fremantle, the ends of this earth.

They caught me in Bristol at a respectable hotel and I had a great deal of property with me but the police could not find what they claimed I had stolen. Those brilliant rings with diamonds. I think it was a case of mistaken identity. I went rowdily and suggested in the strongest possible terms that I was a respectable man who was having his good name sullied by jealous competitors. Not sure I said it in so many words but that was what I believed. And in the court room that fool the tailor burst to the dock and to me and all of the rest of us and demanded that I be charged with stealing his clothes. I got to walk free from that court, acquitted, a man with the problem of a debt.

My belly made up of tongues. Abominable creatures. No, only tongues left, tongues talking, screeching at me and anyone else who wants to hear. It lifts me up, reminding me of my other places. Where I've been. My homes. My sins. His bones are full of the sin of his youth, which shall lie down with him in the dust. Though wickedness be sweet in his mouth, though he hide it under his tongue; Though he spare it, and forsake it not; but keep it still within his mouth: Yet his meat in his bowels is turned, it is the gall of asps within him. He hath swallowed down riches, and he shall vomit them up again: God shall cast them out of his belly. I remember all of the lessons of the holy book.

Krakow Berlin London Fremantle
In those cold prisons. A well travelled man I am. Aren't I? Changeable. My new faces. New names in new places. Books of memories I have of disgust. My sadness, this can't hold together all of it. The threads of a bad life. There were diamond rings and half-boiled potatoes; there were tricks

with petty actions that got me back a little of what I had lost along the way. When I craved a taste I took it. I had enough of wasting time, of losing years and years.

Hush to those tongues. Hush, a peace. Let me think properly. (There are people ahead of me — I can know this, moving forward in time by generations. An eerie, mad thing.)

In my own madness I want to destroy but before this I was only a harmless innocent bloody man.

On the Goldfields I went once with my sons before this being locked up. They called me a Russian (ignorant pigs). Russian Jack. Said I was six foot eight and had never seen anything like me, they said. Said I was one of the finest looking men in the State, broad in proportion to my height, curly haired and bearded, blue eyed. Altogether a magnificent type. I must take their word for all of this. We found some gold with a Russian man not me but a convict who knew about gold from stealing it in England. That was why he was here.

The voice in his belly was a noisy one: it forced him into places he hadn't considered going before. He heard it clear as day; it wasn't just an abstract thing. It moved up from his guts and it spoke to him of horrors. For a short time he thought he had been returned a king: remembering the kings of Israel, remembering how Ehud slashed the guts of Eglon because he was a bad king. He said I have a message from God for you and he thrust his sword into the king's belly so that the hilt followed the blade, and the fat closed upon the hilt; he did not withdraw the sword from the belly, and the contents burst out.

This voice: the sound of its imperfections. The carriage of an asthmatic condition turned into singsong and sometimes bellowing but always this sound coming up, up from the belly and right into the cache of what he knows. The sound of imperfection; always there was an echo, a rasping, gasping for air.

Having the voice so intimately attached made him lonely. A profound solitude this was, a ghostly walk through loss. It was an impediment. One day he decided he must counter this voice and become as loud as he could be. Block out everything with his own formidable sound. That was his control. He had become detached from everything ordinary, even the cadence of a voice in conversation.

Fremantle

There are ghost sightings with the power to stay in a body forever. Carried along by the living and the dead. Moved by a spirit, the residues of earlier lives. I was moved by some sort of spirit over a long hot summer at the Fremantle Arts Centre, housed in the limestone building. The apocryphal story says that Theodore, for all four years as an inmate, had no visitors except the one when a summons was delivered by a creditor.

In the big limestone building that treasures the making of art and craft: a transmutation from loony bin to arts centre. The place where Theodore died. A haunted space up on a hill that looks over the harbour town of Fremantle. The summer spent there was in preparation for a group show of exhibition, performance and installation by women artists, an investigation of the decommissioned gaol and lunatic asylum that had erased the store of knowledge of its female inhabitants. Once the buildings were turned into history museums, they appeared to have become exclusively male sites.

I can feel old Theodore here, because I want to. Didn't really know back then, at the beginning of this search, that he was such a maverick, a trickster. Now I have read about his crimes and his handy work in newspapers and court records. And this means suspending my expectation that they will spell his name correctly. Perhaps it was also the ploy of the trickster, never staying in one place long enough, until he arrived in Australia.

Theodore Krakouer
Teoder Kiakouer
Isidore Theodore Krakerer
Teodor Krakaner
Charles Theodore Krakouer
German. Jew. Pole. Jew. Convict. Russian Jack.

You wouldn't know how mad it was when I first came here it was against my will. Transported from Portland Prison, an age in that rotting gaol. For stealing silks and laces and pretty shawls. Our bodies piled up stinking. Becoming soupy and coming apart on that nasty boat. Second boat to the bloody Swan River. And they weren't ready for us. Some of those poor bastards stayed out there on the boats in the Gage's Roads for months waiting for the gaol to be built, looking into the harbour like poor little fish. Others sent to work to build their own gaol. Cruel bastards. The place ugly and hard, scorching. The only thing to do — play up. Hey ho! Some days I am full of life. Others I'm fully cooked. All I can think of is I hope this ends soon. Please God.

Confusions in my head and in the blood pulsing through me making me skittish and scared. Other times I feel good remembering when there was more to go on more to make me happy. Round and round in a circle and now here I am in the kingdom of the dead. We are all of us dead here and we have monsters feeding off us.

And I'm thinking about love, still. About being in bed with a woman. It doesn't happen here. I'm ugly now. Shitty pants. Spotty dick. Blood. Something bad is wrong with me.

Can't hold it all in.

But before there were smells we would make between the sheets. In the night some women. With me undressed.
My big whole man's body.

My family fatherless now.

At night all comes to life. My dreams. Mother and father. Fears. The darkest fears. Oh god don't tell me again these abominations. Your destructions. Spinning out into anger. Into monsters.

Yes, man I will kill
monster
I would hurt babies and
the order of the natural
world
I can hurt many things
at once
rage monster man
hurtful hurt that
old man
that's a start
that is just the start
I can hear you man
this head hurts
this body is changing

stop it.
Slow down.
I am going as fast as I can I am mad
I am hurt
capable of anything or everything

as a boy I read of the Golem
Monster Man.

Now I am it.

There is a pestilence   these things in my head
in my heart
I'm sick   no relief
feverish
too fast this is hell
they let us yell in here
I will explode   or
die
give me tobacco for my pipe
show me the black backside of the native again
black all over
they call me a nigger
what am I?
not black like that one. Nanyara.

Can I get?
out
a master insistent pressing down on me every night
telling me   over and over
horrible   I never thought such things
before
killing and pulling it all apart
it is the world   and he wants me to do it
be his servant   do it for him he too meek or scared
up on top of this hill   looking down on free-mantle
on the busy town   full of bastards   my children.

Well well here we are and you aren't safe

there's a lion in here for the ladies
a big steel trap for the men   *a bucket for the babies*
fires will roar through after   *the disease has mangled*
anyone left
I will kill   *it must be done*

blood will flow   *and then disaster*
we are finished
a bad idea   *this life.*

There were good and bad convicts everywhere and that is probably why the trade in bodies ceased — it was too hard to make judgements and the community always wanted to do the judging. The colonists asked for a certain type of prisoner. They had a list: no men from Irish prisons; no hardened or serious criminals; none who would lower the moral tone of the colony; no men over forty-five years; no females. They had another list: able-bodied; well-conducted; guilty only of minor offences; with at least half a sentence still to serve. The British sent whomsoever they pleased, although the concession at the start was to send minor criminals to let the colony get used to their new demography; and then later they emptied their gaols of hard cases and sent them out to Western Australia. Changed the offence on the convict papers if they needed to. Almost ten thousand men came in a period of eighteen years, along with Pensioner Guards and their families.[31]

Words are wrapped around the picture. Hundreds of new bodies in the colony, rough-looking men. Everyone here can tell they have been locked up for a long time. These reminders of home, of light deprivation, of poor diets, although the food supply available to the average colonist is not highly nutritious. When these men were despatched from the ship anchored out at Gage Roads and landed on firm ground after one hundred days at sea, they looked perplexed. Probably just getting used to the light at a harsher pitch than the ocean-borne light because it reflected off limestone and sand.

For all the colonists, including these new ones without a choice, there must have been a bedrock of common understandings and shared experiences. Even for the first to land in the colony, those founders. The idea of home, of Britain, of green and pleasant lands, of congested cities, of family and enterprise and, now, of immense travel. And probably, for all of them, the puzzling visage of the black man. Never had they seen anything as "uncivilised".

My words are wrapped around a picture of Theodore in London, looking respectable and being the jewellery merchant; the German Jew who appears in court regularly, who travels around England purposefully. He had no distinguishing features, no tattoos or scars across his face. He was, after all, a *respectable looking German Jew* and a merchant to boot. Although in that decade there was an intense debate about the value or otherwise of the science of phrenology, a debate that continued throughout the century and into the next, there is no evidence that Theodore's skull was measured and any determination on his intelligence handed down.

This thing that happens, just on the edge of consciousness, usually in the responsible spaces of daily life. A blooming of romance, about the family, transmitted as an involuntary picture from memory, a tic. Appearing, reappearing, on the edge of things. Fleeting. Flashes that can catch you unawares. Driving through the city and, suddenly, after all the recent optimism, what you realise you want to do, split-second, is to keep driving, right down and into the river. Coming out of a dream filled with good advice, entwined with a warm and beloved body, and suddenly, there it is. A recognition. Sure to be dismaying: so little there to learn from.

The inheritances of a past become mute, shamed into silence and stupidity. A childhood and then an adulthood without information passed on by family. Without sticks and stones, grand contretemps, noisy tantrums. Any conflict in this family has been patched over and nobody can remember any detail of the reasons for sisters refusing to speak to each other for the rest of their lives, for half a century. Left for dead, or for conjecturing, isolated, curious members of new generations. Like me.

Memory tics offering up outlines of bodies and events, of those stored distresses, complicated sadnesses, and, uncannily, some of the pleasures. Reconstructions of the intricate lives of the people you follow in a family. But also more instructional somehow; from this I want to know about how mistakes, those bad mistakes that teach you nothing after the first time, can be avoided.

family history

I don't want to forget Theodore Krakouer and Brina Israel even if everybody else in the world has. There is so little passed down that I have become a collector of shards: of memory, what might have been told to me at the end of this long line of tales. I want to catch these half-lit, often, paste jewels. I don't know how authentic they are, but does it even matter? For me it doesn't matter because I want to see what can be made anew, built from the remains. To honour the fleeting, the fragment, fractured histories and stories. None of this passed down; it has to be dredged up. On his death certificate it is stated that his brain has gone soft.

I want to give Theodore one of my dreams:

I'm in the loony bin   moving from my bed to the slops room
I've killed Brina and a child   which one   I don't know
stuck them in a cupboard   will I get away with it

or will someone find them?
they'll start smelling for sure — all the matrons and nurses and wardens and that doctor Barnett are walking around the building
together looking investigating
they walk past me
out of the shoulder of one big fat man is the head of a baby
a terrible sight the baby head going crazy
screaming
at me
cat among the pigeons cat among the pigeons —
now they'll know.

This is me:
Man with funny whiskers he's a Russian a Pole a convict a Jew man a handsome man because he's so big — tall and broad that's good in this country — a big broad country Australia with more opportunities than Krakow
London Berlin other places he lived
dealing prospecting exploring belonging with money one day a month making money
wily possibly not to be trusted — he once was a convict he stole clothes in London, England left a wife and son and got himself a new woman and had nine children then he went mad — it was a horrible life.

his display

He went on a rampage through the streets of Fremantle. It wasn't the first time. Yelling, cursing, offending everyone. Hitting himself in his belly, talking in a low growl. He was a frightening sight and he stunk of all the body smells of alcohol and distress and the exertion of trying to escape distress.

He went mad across the vast span of Fremantle town: hot, soaked through with intoxicants, and suffering from base illnesses. He was part of a scene of anarchy. Something so dangerous about drinking alcohol in such a hot climate, the booze cooking up before it even hits the gut.

People knew him but what could they do? Nobody wanted to get involved, get their hands dirty. The language that came from his mouth was foul. Not all of it English, but you could tell it was obscene. People said he had many fluent languages in his head: German, Polish, Yiddish, even Hebrew. And then English, where the foul words came from. Doesn't the facility for more than one language mean the subject is clever? No one treated this man as clever or even as human anymore. He was viewed with caution, like the big packhorses he ran in teams down the Williams Road with provisions and goods required for agriculture. This the business that he once ran; his wife and eldest son now managing matters carefully, cooperating with their customers and always delivering on time.

The police arrive to take him to the limestone palace on the hill that he helped to build. There will be a cell waiting for him in that most popular establishment of a lawless place. Godforsaken Fremantle. 1874.

Where is this man's wife and why can't she control him? Public spectacles like these were best performed later in the day, after the sun went down. Here he was and it was midday, rampaging right through the middle of the town, all the way down to the harbour, the place where he had landed twenty years before.

sins of the fathers

Brina and Theodore's firstborn, Abraham Joseph Krakouer, killed a man in Albany, a town at the bottom of Western Australia. The victim was a bluejacket, a seaman of the HMS *Diamond*. This happened on 2 June 1885 — he "feloniously and wilfully and of his malice aforethought did kill and murder one Henry Rodber against the peace of our Lady the Queen her crown and dignity."[32] Krakouer shot him with a revolver just below his left nipple. The cause of death was sudden haemorrhage from the wound through the heart. The deceased carried a knife but didn't get the chance to use it. The accused was refused bail and the trial was held for three days from Monday 17 August 1885 in the Supreme Court of Western Australia in Perth.

He was a fiercely jealous man and still acting like a newlywed even though it was the fourth year of his marriage to Alicia Catherine née Robinson and there were two babies underfoot and another on the way. It gave him the dry horrors when this ship came in and offloaded its many men. He wasn't thinking straight, he just found that he had lost all confidence in the people around him whether he knew them or not. It was the year that he went a little mad; he dropped all of the defences that had kept him together, that had allowed him to be such a support to his mother and the rest of the family when there had been a world just waiting to be conquered. The business was strong, the other boys were now involved and he had decided to live in Albany to see what it would be like.

With his new bride. And here they were, men who trampled over the town, drank and caroused and acted like they owned the place. He galloped up to a group of them walking towards his house and it made him angry to think they could be as cavalier about the town's space. He had a big fight the night before in the Weld Arms. That was why he was now carrying the revolver. If they came near his house he would shoot them. That was his threat and he meant it so he yelled it at them. These Pommy men were a little taken aback, so one of them asked him if he was an Englishman. When he answered yes this same man said that if he was an Englishman surely he would put down the revolver.

Last night they had all followed him back from the Weld Arms and said they would tear his house down and they had used very bad language in front of his wife. And by now everyone has forgotten what it is they are disputing. The next few minutes are collapsed into chaos with too many people crowding around. First there is Mrs Krakouer speaking with a bluejacket at the gate into the house and all of the men becoming excited with the feeling of something about to happen. And suddenly the young man was speaking to the lady on the verandah with another lady who had just joined them, named Maggie Haggerty, and Krakouer yelling again in a most dramatic way and what seemed from the verandah was that he was baiting this Rodber to enter the house and at the same time yelling "Enter my house and I'll shoot you!" And everyone crowding around. Another bluejacket yelling and yelling to Krakouer and baiting him and saying he would shake the liver out of him. Krakouer yelling out "You all want to eat me!" And Rodber climbing up onto the verandah and his mates pulling him back and Mrs Krakouer pushing him. And then following the bait and stepping into the house, three steps and Krakouer saying "Look what you did with my nose you tore it half off" and Rodber saying "What about my eye and sorry about the nose," and Krakouer saying "You rowdy fellows if your Captain says anything tell him to come see me." Ha!

And suddenly Rodber steps back out onto the verandah and swings around and lifts up his arm and he falls down dead and the two shots have been spent and so was a lot of that excitement in the air. Even though many of the men have sticks they don't use them. Krakouer takes his wife now by the arm and they enter into the house and he closes the door and you can hear the bolt sliding across and their footsteps heading up the hall. And then silence. They are a little in shock, they reel away and they pick up Rodber's body once they see he is dead and slowly they take him away up the street and then that is it. What happens behind the closed doors of Krakouer's house after that is a mystery. How words are spoken between him, Abraham, and his wife and the other lady and Mr Newshead, the man who also lives there. And what happens back on the ship with now a dead body and a lot of excited sailors who have been involved in a crime is also not known.

And the following day Krakouer was arrested and charged with Murder. It was his first criminal offence. Abraham Joseph Krakouer was found guilty of manslaughter and sentenced to two years' hard labour. And afterwards he continued in the coach trade in the Eastern Goldfields and became one of the best-known proprietors, and he married two more times and somewhere in between he had a torrid love affair with Ma Thomas, who later became Ma Raine, and after they had been together for years it is said that he suddenly married her sister. He and Ma Thomas ran the Wentworth Hotel together before he betrayed her, and after that she didn't care for him. He became a saloon owner and ran a saloon in William Street on the other side of the bridge and another one in Murray Street which was the same street as the Wentworth Hotel. During the days when he was still in favour with Ma Thomas, she kept his portrait hanging behind the reception desk in the foyer of the big hotel. He died in 1928 at the Perth Public Hospital. He made his Last Will and Testament one month before he died and he named as his executor Elizabeth Gertrude Keyser, 108

Herbert Road, West Subiaco, married woman, who was the widow of his brother Rudolph and now remarried. But she did not fulfil her obligations as executor and a note on the official record states: *abandoned*. His short Obituary describes him as *the first Jewish baby born in the Colony.*

Broomehill: the start of the story

the start of love

I began to write my stories about Perth and Fremantle, about my family and their arrival here, in the inner suburbs of the nation's capital. Canberra, a cold-hearted place, a city that empties out at Christmas and every other holiday when people return to where they belong, or once belonged, or still wish they belonged. I found I couldn't write as I had been yearning to about the intriguing coincidences and rambling stories I had been collecting: they seemed to require a bodily attachment, or maybe the new place was to blame. I was collecting details from the National Library and realising that I was yearning to write it in Perth.

I was comforted by the one photograph album I had carried with me, its contents showing the record of my growth, and the imprint of my parents. The shared features in a smaller form in the photographs that plot my development through all of the volumes of albums. The genetic stamp marking me as unmistakably theirs and showing the shape of things to come. Sitting next to parents a feature can be shown in duplicate: the ski-jump nose; the thickness of ankles; a most unusual shade of auburn hair. On the adult it looks sophisticated, on the child precocious. It will take a decade or more to grow into the look.

Broome

We arrive in the town at night full of the flurry of farewells and into a sealed air-conditioned compound with two-blanket beds. Until the next day or the following one we are unaware that the heat will be as shocking as it is. Hotter than we have anticipated, a different sort of heat. We, at least, have the refuge of air-conditioning, always set too cold, a rarity in the town. Broome. 1968. I am a child; I am ten years old when we come to this place. It is such a great opportunity for us that I could already tell before we stepped onto the Fokker Friendship plane that we will be changed people after it. So far, our life has been contained; we have lived modestly in three different houses and I have attended two schools, but still I am shy and not experienced in the world. From now on, everything will be different; that was the promise made by those we leave behind. The father is no longer a footballer; now we are in the hospitality business. This is to be a gregarious life.

We are living in the Continental Hotel, a grand old wooden Broome hotel with wide verandahs and a series of courtyards. We take all of our meals in the dining room with hotel guests, sitting as a family unit, mother, father and two little girls with very good manners. Sometimes other people will sit with us, and the waitresses will always joke with us and make us comfortable. The table is set formally, with heavy silver water jugs, starched linen, a typed menu. *Good evening Miss White, Hello, Miss Vera.* We call all of the staff Mr, Mrs or Miss.

This is our new life: it is a public life, a not-domestic life. To be envied by other children who are forced to eat what is put in front of them every night and then make their beds before school each morning. The only beds we make are during school holidays when we help the housemaid with her round of occupied rooms for some extra pocket money. We have come here from Perth, still a small city enclosed and closed-off by its fear of differences, a city of xenophobic inclinations. We have come to live here and for my parents to be the bosses of the hotel. In Broome we find an expansiveness in every sense. The domestic life of our family has changed, and so has our sense of space. We roam here; all the time travelling, on the backs of our horses, or further out with stays on cattle stations and into other towns. Here we come to know new things. The first day at school is an awakening. There are black kids, Chinese and Malay kids, and white kids. And plenty who seem to be impossible to pin down in this way. That is one key to the absence of explicit prejudice: when there are so many grey areas, it is hard to categorise and set up hierarchies. This is not the first time I have met kids who aren't white like me: not really, but it feels like it when we are in almost equal numbers.

Broome is steeped in historical fact and celebration as the exemplary multicultural Australian country town. Yet it is also a place where racism seethes. The harmony in the everyday rhythms of the town is undercut with this encoded violence, sanctioned in certain circles and whispered about in others, but it seems that opponents did not have voices brave enough to be heard.

This is the start of my new life where hotels, and then bookshops and libraries, become the markers: they will teach me how to read the world. Spines along a row, drunks down the stretch of a bar, the Dewey system of categories. Children who grow up in hotels and not suburban houses often find each other later on, and compare family life — the splendour or squalor. There are two cathedrals of commitment: the bar and the bookshop. For the customer anyway. Always such a passion for the contents and the philosophy behind the collection by customers and would-be customers; the material of commerce. I was hooked in by the idea of selling books when I stepped into Frances Steloff's *Gotham Book Mart* in New York at twenty-three. That was the age she was when she established it in the 1920s and now she was retired and living upstairs. She came down while I was in there and I decided that I would be a bookseller. That I would collect the secrets of my customers in Perth: what they read, what they desired. And I did, later. Out of that I ranged wider and into the territory of family.

So I decide that the first story I will start with is mine: how I was formed and where I belong. It takes a little fortitude to absorb the details from history, the exclusions and hardships of those who came before me that have not been part of my life. In attempting to return to these stories, I come to a conclusion that I may have to invent most of it.

Starting by thinking that these snapshots are all from my lifetime, nothing much from before I was born. But now I remember those delicate photographic accounts of family life. It doesn't even matter about the drudgery that was probably in each day; these are snaps that introduce glamour. Three photographs. My mother with her father on her wedding day, looking like Audrey Hepburn in her fine-boned glamour, her lovely dress, her ankles unlike anyone else's in the family. They look as though they could snap into two pieces. My mother with my father at their engagement, and then later in the photograph in that fairytale dress that accentuates the lines across her shoulders. My father with an eye to fashion; it's 1958 and he is wearing a tie with jive-dancing figures painted onto it. This looks like a moment of pause before they begin a big party. When their vows are complete there will be another celebration. Somewhere, filed away, there must be sets of proofs that other couples married and bore children and saw them off into the world. That they haven't ever been seen by anyone else does not mean they are not kept as precious by someone.

the historical quest

First there was Broome and later there is Broomehill. Places in which to learn about family; about being in a larger team or excluded from it. In Broome my family wrote itself into a history and convivial relations as hoteliers; in the next town I ran my tongue across the traces that were left of the family. That was all there was.

There was a transformative moment in my family saga and it happened this way. A weekend away from home in two towns named Katanning and Broomehill to pay homage to dead people who had done some good deeds. It is 1993. The Broomehill Historical Society has been planning a centenary celebration for at least twelve months to honour the men involved in forging the Holland Track as an invaluable passage between the Wheatbelt and the Goldfields. It was opened up during the gold rush of 1893 and it took them about six months in the bush to complete their task. Two of the four men who took that journey are my kin: my great-grandfather David Krakouer and his brother Rudolph, who was the leader.

We had organised a contingent, including two of David's daughters, the second eldest, Aunty May, and the youngest, the only ones still living. I travel with my family and we stay in a motel in Katanning. A motel room that holds all the smells of the life that had been there before us, and more fleas and bedbugs than the six adults sleeping in its three rooms can cope with. We don't sleep well.

The next morning we drive the thirty minutes to Broomehill. In a full day's proceedings of dedicating speeches and installing plaques, proceedings we are ill-prepared for by a night of scratching and tossing and turning in our motel beds, there is a recognition that here, in the historical time I live in, many of the practices of the past seem to come together and subtle exclusions are enacted.

We are gathered together in a shire hall where soup and roast chicken meals are served to us. It may be that nobody else in the room notices the revision of the story being told, or maybe they don't think it is worth mentioning. The Krakouer men were in every way as important as the other two on the expedition: it is said that Rudolph bankrolled it. But in the speeches, in the acknowledgements, and in the plaques that spelt their surname incorrectly, was this marking out, this judgement. And it read to me as a rollcall: sons of convicts, Jewish, merchants, outsiders. And, possibly, the most important impediment to a full celebration was the legacy of just how many Aboriginal people in the area have this same Polish name that means *of Krakow*. One hundred years after the event, to the day, their compatriots Mr Holland and Mr Carmody, fellow explorers, were celebrated for bearing the responsibility and heroism of the six-month journey. There we were, proud of our two men, the largest family gathering in the big Broomehill hall. The message was diminishing: there was something lesser in the effort of David and Rudolf Krakouer because of *who* they were.

Surveillance entails pleasure. I am an inveterate spy and this is how I started on the family. The ways and means of collecting data are most appealing, so I go through presentation chocolate boxes and files in bottom drawers, and I construct a case. Read intimate letters that perhaps should never have been kept. Find references in books that were published back in the 1920s, a time for recognising the achievements of the pioneers.

> The early manhood of the late Rudolph Krakouer, a West Australian native, was spent in the Williams and Kojonup districts ... a great athlete in the early 'eighties — champion runner, a prominent footballer, and cricketer, and a crack

> shot with the rifle. Physically a fine man — he stood 6ft. 2in. in height, and was built in proportion — a genial and kindly disposition, he was well liked by his fellow men. "A white man" was how he was described.
>
> Just before the Goldfields came to life, he was established at Broomehill on the Great Southern line, having built up a sound drapery and grocery business, and buying sandalwood, skins, etc., locally. In fact "Rude Krakouer" was a household name in the South-west. Of a brave, adventurous spirit, he was one of the very earliest prospectors at Coolgardie, Hannan's, and other fields. Leaving his business in charge of a younger brother, he was claimed by the Goldfields henceforth. After a short time prospecting, he returned to Broomehill, and formed and financed a party consisting of himself, John Holland, and two lads, namely Carmody and his youngest brother David Krakouer. With a team of horses, and provisions, the party, although very often short of water, cut a new track from Broomehill to Coolgardie. After some weeks of hardship they reached Coolgardie. *En route* they named Mount Holland, Lake Carmody and Krakouer's Rocks, which are well known today.[33]

But soon enough and sure enough they changed the names, and now there are no *Krakouer's Rocks*. And changed the spirit of the adventure, an exploration that meant that the gold rush could proceed at full tilt. The Holland Track was consecrated as a noble pioneering task in the history of Western Australia.

the end of it all

By the end of the century all of the panics are back in evidence. Circulating across the nation, racist sentiments try for a clever line in stringently denying they are racist. It's all about economics and the return of the repressed, people say. It seems somehow too late to be having such rudimentary debates about immigration control now that the nation has been *founded* upon difference and a policy of multiculturalism. But they happen, and some Australians come to blows and behave badly and the country is excited by discussions of what is being said about us in the rest of the world.

The isolations involved in being the first white people to settle here don't seem to have left our psyche. We are hindered by this and it weakens every resolve we might have. All I want to do is to reclaim a little space in a town that was governed in every sense by Scottish men, a place where public office was often a matter of birthright and some lucky fathers and sons could work productive partnerships. That is the extent of my dispute about being excluded; it is a modest request, really.

The predictable patterns of the generations. We intend

to improve ourselves and sometimes we do. The photographs we took of each other, those that aren't blurred beyond any ability to recognise, show us wasted by more than substances, legal and illegal. Wasted by opportunity too, with that broadening of education, careers, indulgence. Before that, skinny kids who roamed the streets to catch the bus to the footy, and the beach. Driving on Sundays around the flash suburbs, looking at the houses and the river, spying on Alan Bond's first family home in Nedlands. That one was a favourite for some of us. A very long block down to the river with ponies grazing at the front every Sunday. Sometimes they were being ridden, sometimes waiting. We only did our sightseeing on the weekend so we never knew if the ponies lived on that block or were transported in for the children.

And here are these Krakouers, forgotten by even their forebears. So what? History is a discipline of selection and we weren't chosen. The details of single lives illuminate the family, but briefly. Achievements or talent or infamy are all singular and cannot be claimed by the collective. The story of this family is enmeshed within the story of Australia but to prove all of it is beyond anyone's charter. It contains shameful records, neglected or unacknowledged. Figures rush out of the landscapes and they are not always Krakouers.

There is always a rest of the world and we are never in it.

outside

My bed my centre of a small hotel room in a foreign city with an ornate antique mirror at its head. It is supposed to make the room appear bigger but I am here alone and all I occupy is an edge of the bed. I follow one path back and forwards to the bathroom. That's all. The room big enough for me.

This mirror begins to attract me. Through nights laden with a certain memory, in a realm of lost things, I come to rely on glimpsing myself as I turn from side to side in an approximation of sleep. It comes in my peripheral vision, my face; always with a trace of something else. Watching and being watched in the half-light, half-sleep, I am tempted and captivated and sometimes aroused. Looking intently, for longer than usual, elevated on my elbow, looking on in a wide frame, wider and for once not localised. A reverie for these nights and then days as I become my lover, my face carrying all the ways I have been touched, caressed, changed. The hands and faces of these others I have known and been as close to as this.

I spend all of this time — minutes on end in those precious hours of sleeping — thinking about you and how you might have looked at me. I carry my markings of having been loved. We travelled together through three states of Australia, and promised many more destinations. Mostly we forgot about the rest of the world. Everything an illusion, perhaps.[34]

My interest eliciting a certain sympathy for the way we were and the way those I am now surrounded by are, these other hotel guests with no inhibitions, who do not care about noise, peculiarities in digestive systems, lovemaking, brawls, those regularising patterns of everyday order. In the garish room there is other music, the compact discs of the well-prepared traveller, listened to over and again as if for comfort.

> Porous with travel fever, but you see I'm so glad to be on my own. It's just that the slightest touch of a stranger can send a trembling in my bones.[35]

Everything contingent, I make my way out with the night's newest markings, streaky stains that will one day be scars, and investigate the new city thoroughly.

Notes

1 A O Neville, Chief Protector of Aborigines in Western Australia 1915–40, held many controversial opinions and acted on some of them. Anna Haebich writes of him in *For Their Own Good*:

> During the early 1930s he adopted an increasingly extreme position on the "half-caste" problem, advocating the breeding out of the "coloured population" altogether. (280)

2 Quoted in Ewers, p 11.

3 Census (Colonial Secretary's Office). Perth: Government Press, 1854.

4 C T Stannage refers to these families in *The People of Perth*, p 200. The reference describes the 1888 Perth by- election campaign:

> And behind the government and the *West Australian* were the "Six Hungry Families", all of whom were "shoddy, mean and conceited, and kept from the working men what was rightfully theirs".

5 This period of upheaval and politicisation in Australian health has been well documented in feminist scholarship and in recent histories of the health system in Australia. In *Damned if We Do: Contradictions in Women's Health Care*, Dorothy Broom writes:

> Several of the women involved in the original Perth (Women's Health and Community) Centre were at pains to point out to me that they had been conventional, middle-class, married women with children when they first became involved with women's health care. By the time a crisis reached its peak and funding was withdrawn about eighteen months after the Centre opened, the women had been fundamentally changed by their experiences. Largely unaware of their own transformation, they

found that what they had come to think of as normal and appropriate behaviour was regarded by other women in the community and by government officers as radical. As one woman put it, "We didn't realise how unrespectable we had become." Another observed that they had, almost unwittingly, gone "a little beyond the Pap smear stage." Although the process may have been more dramatic in Perth than in some other cities, the work of women's health centres undoubtedly makes a profound difference to the lives of the workers as well as to clients. (14)

6 See Estelle Blackburn's account of the Eric Edgar Cooke serial murder terror during the 1960s, *Broken Lives*. She makes a strong argument for the incidents and fear marking the "loss of innocence" of Perth.

7 The idea of the concealed pregnancy and the subsequent birth that is denied is not surprising because of the shame involved. C T Stannage, in *The People of Perth*, recounts this story:

> When a Josephine Princep or a Mrs Brittain lost a child in infancy, the pain, fear, and horror experienced was intense and often long-lasting in its effects. But it is also true that it took place within their own home, attended by a doctor who was often a family friend, and with husband and family close by to ease the pain and aid recovery. This was qualitatively different from the experience of a Catherine Kelly. Catherine Kelly arrived at the Servants' Home in 1862, having come out on the *Mary Harrison* with 150 other girls. Catherine became pregnant. Knowing that pregnancy would reduce her chances of gaining employment she did her best to conceal her condition. Her fellow inmates "suspected that she was in the Family way", but it was just talk among the women, for Catherine herself never said a word. On Tuesday 16 September, just after 2 o'clock in the afternoon, having cooked and eaten lunch and feeling ill, Catherine crossed the yard to the privy. As she sat over the pit-hole her baby slid out and down into the cess-pit. When the cord had reached its full length it strained against and then tore from her body, causing the baby to sink into the pit where it died. Catherine dealt with the afterbirth as best she could, and pushed the blood-soiled skirt and rag into the pit also. She looked out from the

closet and saw that some male prisoners were working in the yard. Only when they had moved away did she leave the closet and stagger with Mary Haggerty's support across to the cookhouse where she slumped down. One of the other girls ran to Matron Annear who came quickly and asked Catherine what the matter was. The girl replied that "Nothing was the matter." Matron Annear asked her what she had done. Catherine said that she had done nothing. She hung her head and began to cry.

> Catherine Kelly was first charged with the wilful murder of her child. She faced the Coroner's Court which found evidence only for a charge of concealment of the birth, on which charge she was indicted to appear before the Supreme Court of Western Australia in January 1863. Found not guilty, she was set free to return to the Servants' Home. Here then was a life experience within the embrace of the investing class yet apart from them. It was always the same for the Catherine Kellys of Perth. (114)

What is surprising to me is that into the next century such a lack of basic compassion is still evident.

8 Government Gazette 801.

9 Aborigines Department files 38/27: Police Report 1735/27.

10 *New York Times, 26* May 1942, 3:1 p 56.

11 Bruce Muirden, *The Puzzled Patriots*, p 43.

12 Quoted in Muirden, p 155.

13 ibid., p 84.

14 ibid., p 88.

15 David Horton, ed. *Encyclopedia of Aboriginal Australia,* p 704.

16 The speech can be found on the web site:
www.keating.org.au/searchframe.htm

17 P R Stephensen, *The Foundations of Culture in Australia*, p 12.

18 ibid., p 12.

19 Haebich, p.364.

20 This is from my private correspondence from Ross White, my father's cousin. He later recanted and re-remembered, after more than fifty years, that hers was a name other than Krakouer and sheepishly informed me of his mistake. He remains, however, wavering between the names of the customers he stored during his employment next door to Josie Bungalow and his desire to provide me with a family link.

21 C T Stannage ed., *A New History of Western Australia*, p 174.

22 Stannage, *The People of Perth*, p 12.

23 ibid., *The People of Perth*, p 96.

24 David Mossenson, *Hebrew, Israelite, Jew*, p 10.

25 Pamela Statham, "Origins and Achievements", p 39.

26 Lazarus Morris Goldman. *The Jews in Victoria in the Nineteenth Century*, p 223.

27 Court of Quarter Sessions.

28 Surgeon's Day Journal 1874.

29 25 September 1857.

30 I have borrowed heavily regarding Jewish ritual and reminiscences from Kugelmass and Boyarin.

31 Statham, "Origins and Achievements", p 39.

32 *Albany Mail*, 16 June 1885.

33 Jules Raeside, *Golden Days*, p 197.

34 Title of a painting by Dorothea Tanning (1910 —), Foundation Jean Miro permanent collection, Barcelona.

35 Joni Mitchell, "Hejira" on *Hejira*, Elektra/Asylum Records, New York, 1976.

Bibliography

Official Publications

Court of Quarter Sessions — Portsmouth Borough, Hants. Assizes 25. Indictments 1849, Epiphany December. Ref: S 8/5. Hampshire County Council Records, Great Britain.

Official publications held in State Archives, J S Battye Library of West Australian History, Perth:

Annual Reports of the Aborigines Department, 1927. AN 1/7 ACC993 38/27 City of Perth — Prohibited Area. Police Report 1735/27.

Colonial Secretary's Office Records, Incoming and Outgoing Correspondence, 1873. Accession 50 and 51. Volume 744/178 183.

Colony of Western Australia. Census of 1854 (Colonial Secretary's Office). Perth: Government Press, 1854.

Convict Transportation Registers Australian Joint Copying Project (AJCP). Reel 92 HO11/16. *Mermaid.* 30 December 1850.

Department of Corrections, Convict Registers Character Book. Western Australia, 1852. Accession 1156 R17. 232: Theodore Krakouer.

Fremantle Lunatic Asylum Archives: Admission Book 1857-96; Case Book; Medical Journals; Registers. AN 200.

Government Gazette, 18 March 1927.

Passenger Lists of the *Travancore.* Accession 115/7.

Supreme Court Criminal Sittings, Western Australia. Indictments: Item 129 Case 2116, August 1885.

Surgeon's Journal of *Mermaid.* Surgeon Superintendent Alex Kilroy. Australian Joint Copying Project. Reel M7111.

Newspapers and periodicals

Albany Mail, 16 June 1885.

Perth Gazette, 25 September 1857.
New York Times, 26 May 1942, 3:1. 24 June 1942, 4:7.
The Times. London. 12 October and 18 October 1848.

Electronic sites

Keating, Paul, the Hon. Prime Minister. 10 December 1992, International Human Rights Day, Redfern Park, Sydney. Australian launch of the United Nations International Year for the World's Indigenous People. *http://www.keating.org.au/searchframe.htm*

Books

Aveling, Marian, ed. *Westralian Voices: Documents in Western Australian Social History*. Nedlands: University of Western Australia Press, 1979.

Bell, Diane, and P Hawkes. *Generations: Grandmothers, Mothers, Daughters*. Fitzroy: McPhee Gribble/Penguin, 1987.

Bignell, Merle. *First the Spring: A History of the Shire of Kojonup*. Nedlands: University of Western Australia Press, 1971.

Blackburn, Estelle. *Broken Lives*. Perth: Steller Publications, 1998.

Broom, Dorothy H. *Damned if We Do: Contradictions in Women's Health Care*. Sydney: Allen and Unwin, 1991.

Cameron, J M R, and E K G Jaggard. *Western Australian Readings*. Perth: Churchlands College, 1977.

Connolly, Anthony. "White City: A Critical Legal History of the Prohibited Area Proclamation and Pass System in the Perth Area 1927–1954". Honours Dissertation. Law Library, The University of Western Australia, 1991.

Crowley, F K. *Australia's Western Third*. London: Macmillan, 1960.

Drewe, Robert. *Fortune*. Sydney: Picador, 1986.

Erickson, Rica. *The Brand on His Coat: Biographies of Some Western Australian Convicts*. Nedlands: University of Western Australia Press, 1983.

Ewers, John K. *The Western Gateway*. Fremantle: Fremantle City Council, 1948.

Ferguson, Russell, et al. *Out There: Marginalization and Contemporary Culture*. Boston: Massachusetts Institute of Technology Press, 1990.

Frost, Lucy. *No Place for a Nervous Lady: Voices from the Australian Bush.* Melbourne: McPhee Gribble/Penguin, 1984.

Gibson, Ross. *The Bond Store.* Sydney: Museum of Sydney, 1996.

Goldman, Lazarus Morris. *The Jews in Victoria in the Nineteenth Century.* Self published, Melbourne, 1956.

Haebich, Anna. *For Their Own Good.* Nedlands: University of Western Australia Press, 1989.

Hasluck, Alexandra. *Unwilling Emigrants: A Study of the Convict Period in Western Australia.* Sydney: Angus and Robertson, 1969.

Hassam, Andrew. *Sailing to Australia: Shipboard Diaries by Nineteenth-Century Emigrants.* Melbourne: Melbourne University Press, 1995.

Horne, Donald. *Readers' Digest: The Story of the Australian People.* Sydney: Readers' Digest, 1985.

Horton, David, ed. *Encyclopedia of Aboriginal Australia.* Canberra: Australian Institute of Aboriginal and Torres Straits Islander Studies Press, 1994.

Kugelmass, J, and Boyarin, J, eds. *From a Ruined Garden: The Memorial Books of Polish Jewry.* (2nd edn.) Bloomington: Indiana University Press, 1998.

Kuhn, Annette. *Family Secrets: Acts of Memory and Imagination.* London: Verso, 1995.

Mander, A E. *The Making of the Australians.* Melbourne: Georgian House, 1958.

Maushart, Susan. *Sort of a Place Like Home: Remembering the Moore River Settlement.* Fremantle: Fremantle Arts Centre Press, 1993.

McMahon, P T. *They Wished Upon a Star.* Perth: Service Printing Co., 1972.

Mossenson, David. *Hebrew, Israelite, Jew: The History of the Jews in Western Australia.* Nedlands: University of Western Australia Press, 1990.

Muirden, Bruce. *The Puzzled Patriots: The Story of the Australia First Movement.* Melbourne: Melbourne University Press, 1965.

Nabokov, Vladimir. *Speak, Memory: An Autobiography Revisited.* London: Weidenfeld and Nicholson, 1967.

Ondaatje, Michael. *Running in the Family.* London: Picador, 1985.

Raeside, Jules. *Golden Days.* Perth: Colortype Press, 1929.

Sebald, W G. *The Emigrants*. London: The Harvill Press, 1996.
Stannage, C T, ed. *A New History of Western Australia.* Nedlands: University of Western Australia Press, 1981.
—. *The People of Perth.* Perth: Perth City Council, 1979.
Statham, Pamela. "Origins and Achievements: Convicts and the Western Australian Economy". *Westerly* 30.3 (1985): 37-44.
Steedman, Carolyn. *Landscape for a Good Woman.* London: Virago, 1986.
Stephensen, P R. *The Foundations of Culture in Australia.* Sydney: Forward Press, 1936.

Appendix 1
Theodore Krakouer's crimes

A timeline of Theodore Krakouer's career in England and Australia

11 October 1848. *Charles Theodore Krakueri* charged with stealing eight diamond rings valued at 47 pounds.

17 Oct 1848. *Charles Theodore Krokower.* Final examination on charge of stealing diamond rings. Charged in court by Robert Cooper Casper with stealing a suit of clothing.

23 October 1848. *Teodor Krakauer* and Carl Dollman steal goods from Henry Seeling.

1 November 1848. *Isidore Theodore Krakener* indicted for stealing eight rings, valued at 47 pounds. ACQUITTED.

23 December 1848. *Krakauer* & Dollman indicted at Portsmouth Borough Quarter Sessions for stealing from Seeling. Sentenced to fifteen years' transportation.

8 January 1849. Conviction recorded in Portsmouth.

18 February 1849. *Theodore Krakouer* sent to Millbank Prison, London.

31 October 1849. *Theodore Krakouer* sent to Portland Prison, County Dorset.

28 December 1850. *Theodore Krakouer* sent on board *Mermaid*

9 January 1851. *Mermaid* sails from Portsmouth.

13-17 May 1851. *Mermaid* arrives at Fremantle.

12 Sept 1852. Ticket-of-leave granted. Works for Alfred de Letch.

30 October 1852. *Theodore Krakouer* working for self.

15 Sept 1855. Conditional pardon.

10 October 1874. Committed as a Lunatic to the Fremantle Asylum.

18 May 1877. *Theodore Krakouer* dies in Fremantle Lunatic Asylum.

Appendix 2
Newspaper reports of Theodore Krakouer

Each of Theodore Krakouer's crimes reads, from the following news reports, as inventive and playful. I have attached them for that reason. His recidivist streak is represented by two local Perth reports from 1864 that have no resolution — there is no further mention of another trial commital.

The Times, London. 12 October 1848

CLERKENWELL — Charles Theodore Krakueri, a German Jew of respectable appearance, was placed at the bar before Mr. COMBE charged by Mr. George Joseph, diamond merchant and jeweller, of 19 Woodbridge Street, Clerkenwell, with stealing eight diamond rings, value 47/-.

Mr. COMBE said, he would remand the prisoner for a week. [Several persons here rushed forward to exhibit charges against the prisoner.]

Mr. COMBE told them all to attend at the next examination, and he also directed that the 100 weight of sponges, the prisoner's great coats and cape (which answered the description of what the party wore on the day of the robbery) and other articles (if any) should be brought up on Tuesday next. They ought to have been brought in this instance for the prisoner to identify.

Sherwinski said, there would be numerous charges brought against the prisoner, and Mr. Joseph said, that a great many depredations of this sort had lately been committed in Clerkenwell …

The Times, London. 18 October 1848

CLERKENWELL — Charles Theodore Krokower, a German Jew, was placed at the bar for final examination, charged by Mr. George Joseph, diamond merchant and jeweller, of No. 19 Woodbridge street Clerkenwell, with stealing eight diamond rings value 47/-.

The prisoner, it may be recollected, called upon the prosecutor and, representing himself as a merchant in partnership with his brother, inspected some diamond rings, eight of which he selected and ordered to be sealed up in a box, and promised to return for them with the money changed for them; but, before he left the house, he dexterously contrived to substitute another box in lieu of the genuine one containing the rings, bearing an exact resemblance, and as he did not return with the money the box was subsequently opened and found to contain nothing but rags and two half-boiled potatoes. The prisoner was traced and apprehended at Bristol, but none of the property was found.

Benjamin Britton, a Bristol officer, produced a coat and cap which were found at the prisoner's lodgings, and were identified as being those worn by him on the day of the robbery. The prisoner, by the advice of Mr. Sidney, reserved his defence, and he was fully committed for trial on this charge.

The prisoner was then charged by Mr Robert Cooper Casper, tailor, of St. Mary Axe, with stealing a suit of clothes. The prisoner ordered the clothes, which were taken home by the prosecutor, when he put them on and said he could not pay until he got some French notes cashed, and he requested prosecutor to accompany him to a bullion office in Lombard Street. He walked with him as far as King William street, city, where the prisoner entered a house and escaped with the clothes, and he did not afterwards see him until he was in custody at the bar of this court. The clothes were now produced and identified by Mr. Casper. The prisoner was fully committed for trial on this charge.

Other charges of a similar description were preferred against him, but they failed in legal proof; the parties, however, were left to indict at the sessions if they thought proper.

The Inquirer and Commercial News, Perth. 1 June 1864

An order stolen from Phillips, the person who lost the sum of four hundred and ninety pounds in orders a short time since, was presented at Fremantle, and the person who offered it — a man named Krakouer — was arrested; a large sum of money was found on his person, and he informed the police that another man, whom he named, had also a large sum. This person had went to Bunbury, whither the police proceeded and it is hoped that the guilty parties will be brought to justice though there is not much prospect of the money being recovered.

The Inquirer and Commercial News, Perth. 13 July 1864

Theodore Krakouer, who had been arrested on a charge of robbery, was discharged from custody on Friday, the evidence not being sufficiently complete to enable the Crown to prosecute. He was however arrested, after leaving the Court and will most probably be again committed to trial. Another man named Louis Myers, accused of being implicated in the same robbery, and who was out on bail, did not appear when called and his recognizances were entreated. It was said he had left the colony, but he was subsequently captured near Fremantle, and is now in the Perth lock-up. Both these men were apprehended on suspicion of robbing a man named Phillips of a large sum of money at the Wheal Fortune Mine.

Appendix 3
Brina Israel's letters

I include Brina Israel's letters and related correspondence regarding the order to pay for Theodore Krakouer's keep in the lunatic asylum because of their simple eloquence and from the sheer delight of finding handwritten records of my forebears. They have been transcribed from microfiche from the records of the Colonial Secretary's Office, Incoming Correspondence.

~

Perth Poor House
August 30 1873
To Honourable Colonial Secretary Perth

I have the honour to inform you I have this day, on certificate of Resident Magistrate and of this Medical Practitioner admitted Theodore Krakouer as a patient to the Fremantle Asylum.

I have obtained from his son, and now enclose to you an engagement to pay for the maintenance of patient during the time of his confinement as patient.

Mr Dale

~

Sir
Mrs Krakouer has only two children at home 1 boy 10 years old, and a daughter younger. Mrs Krakouer keeps a shop and attends all sales in town and does a good business by trucking and dealing with Goods — they have a team of Horses and dray which her son Abraham drives as far as the Williams of the Eastern districts takes up goods and brings back produce and besides there is several horses and a dray now at home, and at the present time Abraham is away with one team — both the Son and Mother are shrewd

dealing persons and make out a very good livelihood and are no doubt in good circumstances and require no assistance whatever.

I am, Sir

Your obedient

~

Perth Poor House
August 20th 1874
The Honourable
The Colonial Secretary

Sir
I beg to state, in July I made enquiries into Mrs Krakouer's circumstances and ability to pay for her Husband's support in this Lunatic asylum. I found that she had leased a piece of land from Mr Hammersley at the Williams and put up a house on the same which she intends to use as a Store, that she also has two good Teams employed on the Road between the Williams and Perth and to all appearances doing a good business.

I myself heard her say a short time since her credit was so good in Fremantle that if she required goods she could have them to the amount of 1000 pounds, I consider she is well able to pay for her husband's support and will not if she can by any means avoid it.

I have the honour to be
Sir
Your Most obedient servant
W Dale
Officer in Charge

~

Fremantle 26.12.1873

Sirs
(the first line indecipherable) … I was afraid & that if I thought for fear I could get him in the Lunatic Asylum not looking to part with

him as he is quite harmless I went in the country with him to first in attending to his business when we got near Mooroombine? He left me & was lost in the bush four days & nights without food or drink I gave notice to a police constable & when he was found I sent him to Fremantle with my son the doctors then gave my son certificates to get him in the Asylum which cost us three guineas he was kept in for a few weeks Dr Waylen & Dr Barnett examined him while I was in the country & discharged him he was not out of the Asylum one hour before a great many people could see he was worse than ever. My daughter was in charge of the housekeeping, frightened, made an application to Mr Slade & to Dr Barnett. They of course could do nothing for him unless she paid again for certificates which of course she could not do. Mr Slade told her if he committed himself in any way he would be taken in which of course he did in the following way. He went into the house of a woman who I think could not be of very good character & he sent for beer for her she would not give him any change of the money he gave her so he took two common tumblers & told her he would summons her for the rest. He brought them away openly in the day time & when the constable came for him he told him the same as he told others. My daughter wishing him — advised him to go to the station house. He then told Mr Slade he would not be tried by him. Mr S then committed him for trial he has been in the Lunatic asylum ever since I am sorry to say worse than ever The Doctors can testify to that. The Sister was being summoned to attend the sessions against him. I think it is a great pity that he should be took to Perth in his present state & myself with such a large helpless family to support. I wish to spare all the expenses I can I have therefore taken the liberty of writing to you & begging a favourable answer as soon as convenient.

I remain

your obedient servant.

B Krakouer

~

Fremantle 18.9.1874

Sir

My husband as you are aware is now a Lunatic in the Asylum. I am now left with a large & helpless family to support with only the assistance of my eldest son a Lad of 20 years of age. He is trying his best to keep me & my family out of the Poor House & I hope with God Almighty's help to be able to keep out of it. I have already been there twice & that is quite sufficient for me. My husband suffered a great deal of unnecessary trouble as you are well aware. God forbid I should say it was that brought him where he is. I should not trouble you with this only I am afraid my son & myself will be affected in the same manner. If we are to be the — when all considered they are making a very good beginning some time back I had the honour of receiving a letter from you stating the law must take its course with my husband. He was committed for summons the bill was thrown out that first day of the occasions on the 1st of September he was admitted in the Lunatic Asylum in September. He was sent out of it in October. He was committed for trial to be tried in January they have now sent me in a bill for his keep in the Lunatic Asylum on the 1st of September to the 31st of December which of course there is no claim. there is only one thing I have to ask you that is begging that my Husband becomes a free inmate of the Asylum. in fact it would be trespassing too much on your valuable time in telling you how I am served there is one thing favourable in the public sympathy within my truly unfortunate position & I can only trust that you will do the same & you will find that I will never transgress the Law. I only want fair play. I would be very glad if you allow me to see you at any time or would think proper to me. Begging your pardon for troubling you.

I am yours obediently.

B Krakouer

~

The Hon F P Barlee Esq

Sir
I would not trouble you only I am duty bound according to my own conscience & the advice of my friends to contradict such a base falsehood that has been told to you & I think I ought to know the author of such an untruth. What I write to you the inhabitants of Fremantle can prove. I only wish the person that gave you the information would take my ample means & support my Husband & my self & children. I would be truly grateful & so would my Husband's creditors for there is a good many of them in this place. When my Husband was first put into the Asylum the bailiff immediately afterwards came in to the house. My Husband owes a great deal of money which can be provided. I am paying them all a little at the time on purpose to keep my few belongings together to enable my son & myself to try & get a living for ourselves without becoming a burden upon government. The public know the unnecessary trouble my poor Husband was often put to. No wonder that he ends his days in a Lunatic Asylum. I am afraid that my son will be driven there too unless I have the means to send him out of the Colony & then perhaps Government will be kind enough to keep my children & me for already one of Krakouer's creditors not satisfied to wait has sent a summons to the Lunatic asylum. Poor fellow they wont let him rest there. I would feel obliged if you would grant me an interview as I wish to speak to you. Please name the time that will suit your convenience.

Yours obediently.
B Krakouer

~

August 21 1874
To the Honorable Colonial Secretary

Sir
I can scarcely express my feelings when unfortunately I have to mention the circumstances connected with my Husband now in

the Lunatic Asylum. I have been applied to pay for the keep of my Husband a sum now which unfortunately to say is not in my power to pay How willing I should have been to do so had I not been left with a large helpless family & the only dependence I have is in my eldest son a lad of twenty years of age who has to work very hard to support us (Most people say great credit is due to him) Too much put on him must be the cause of him wishing to leave the colony. He my son is willing or am I if we can get some assistance from Government to send my Husband home to his native country to his relatives in Berlin for the present it is as much as we can do to keep out of the poor House — should business prosper I should only be too happy to offer the support of my Husband — at present I must beg the release of any payment demanded of me & my son. I therefore hope & pray Sir you will be good enough to intercede on my behalf & I will be ever grateful. I am now living in Perth & if you will allow me the honour of an interview with you I will explain more fully to you how I am situated & will give you ample proofs if required.

Your very humble & obedient servant

B Krakouer

Acknowledgements

Thanks to:

My family for their support, particularly to my mother Andrea, father Alan, sister Natalie, and Bruce, Tina and Wayne.

Special thanks to Barbara Milech for her unstinting support. Thanks too to Brian Dibble for the same.

Generous spirited friendship and inspiration from Gail Jones, Marion Campbell, Daniel Brown, Joan London, Elizabeth Jolley, Julie Lewis, Carmen Lawrence, Tom Flood and Sharon Jones, Kathleen Mary Fallon, Rosslyn Prosser, Susan Varga and Anne Coombs, Kate Lamont, and Terry Pitsikas.

Thanks to Angela Rockel for her metaphor and enthusiasm; Ross White, second cousin, for his interest; Maude Bonshore, cousin, for her assistance. And Loreley Morling for her genealogical work.

trAce, the International Writing Community, and *anat*, the Australian Network of Arts and Technology, offered me many opportunities with an on-line writing residency in Nottingham, England, in 1998.

I wish to acknowledge the receipt of an Australia Council

project grant in 1995, and an ArtsWA project grant in 1998, both of which offered me time and space at early stages of the writing. Thank you to Varuna Writers' Centre and the Eleanor Dark Foundation for the brilliant space to write in 1999, and the chance to borrow from Eleanor Dark's personal library.

During 1998 and 1999 I had the chance to present aspects of my work to a number of Jewish organisations in Perth. Their support and feedback was enormously helpful.